SON

OF

PERDITION

A Leviathan Publication

Leviathan | Marin County, California

Cover art by Tim Bradstreet

© Tim Bradstreet

Used with permission

Cover design by Rob Ozborne

www.robozborne.com

FIRST TRADE PAPERBACK ORIGINAL EDITION

ISBN-13: 978-0692184561

ISBN-10: 0692184562

For Sean Cleveland. With gratitude.

"War is cruelty. There is no use trying to reform it. The crueler it is, the sooner it will be over."
— General William Tecumseh Sherman

"Because you did not serve the Lord your God with joyfulness and gladness of heart, because of the abundance of all things, therefore you shall serve your enemies whom the Lord will send against you, in hunger and thirst, in nakedness, and lacking everything. And he will put a yoke of iron on your neck until he has destroyed you."
— Deuteronomy 28:47-48

"I am the devil, and I'm here to do the devil's business."
— Charles "Tex" Watson

TUESDAY

Samuel Glazer spent two days watching the farm, studying the family's movements, when they left, when they fed the animals, when they took supper. It was an hour or so after sunrise and Glazer was crouched low in a small ravine on the west side of the farm, hidden behind some brush. His hair was matted and tangled, his shirt starched stiff with dried sweat. Despite the early hour, it was already hot and thin beads of sweat ran down his forehead, carving salty paths through the layer of dirt on his face.

The farm was owned by a man named Harold Camp. The property was small, roughly twenty acres of grazing land along with a modest house, a barn, and a dilapidated pen that held several hogs. Both the barn and the house were in a state of slow decay and neither had ever been painted, the wood stained from years of rain and wind. One of the windows on the house was gone, replaced by a thin piece of cowhide, the corners nailed into what was left of the window's frame. The earth in front of the house was littered with small patches of dead grass and deep ruts caused by wagon wheels rolling through mud.

Glazer pulled a small piece of paper and a bit of whittled lead out of his shirt pocket. The paper had eight names on it, two of which were already crossed off. Glazer licked the lead and drew a straight line through Harold Camp's name. He had seen what he needed to see. He put the paper and lead back into his pocket.

The front door of the house banged open and Harold came outside, a cigarette hanging from his mouth. He wore a pair of filthy overalls and he walked over to the hogs, looked inside for a moment, and went for the barn. A moment later, he led out an old horse and hooked it to the wagon. He climbed up into the seat and slapped the horse with the reins. The horse moved slowly, its breathing labored. The pigs started to grunt and squeal, wanting to be fed.

Harold moved down the lane, toward the road that led to Whitwell. As the wagon disappeared from sight, Glazer lifted his rifle up off the ground and sighted it in on the front door of the house. He knew that Harold would probably hear the shots, but the road was narrow and the horse was old. There was plenty of time.

It was nearly ten minutes before Harold's wife Dorothy came outside. Glazer fired. The shot took her directly in the stomach, the bullet blowing out her back and ricocheting off the front of the house. Dorothy collapsed in a heap, her right hand clutching her bleeding gut. Glazer stayed in the ravine, the rifle once again aimed at the door.

The front door slammed open as Harold's only child, a boy in his teens, came running out. Glazer didn't know his name. The boy went for his mother and Glazer shot him in the shoulder. The kid spun around like a top and his feet tangled and he fell to the ground. Glazer checked the road before leaving the ravine. He walked across a large patch of fallow ground toward the wife and kid. The kid was struggling to reach his mother, his left arm hanging uselessly at his side. The boy's face was smeared with dirt and blood, and tears rolled down his cheeks. The ground beneath him was stained a thick red.

Glazer reloaded the Spencer as he walked toward them. The boy looked up and saw him, a fierce wild man of sweat and filth storming out of the brush, and he knew that this was the end. He ceased his lame crawling and simply stared.

Glazer slung his rifle and looked down at the boy. "I'll be back for you," he said.

He grabbed Dorothy by the arms and dragged her toward the pig pen. Saliva trickled out of her mouth as she struggled to stay conscious, her mouth flapping like a fish gasping for breath. When they reached the pig pen, he let the woman drop to the ground and opened the gate.

There were five pigs in the pen, four males and a sow. The sow ran toward the gate as it opened and Glazer kicked it hard in the side. It squealed and backed off but stayed within a close radius of the gate, snorting and panting and clawing at the ground.

He grabbed Dorothy under the shoulders and pulled her into the pen, taking care to keep the pigs away, swinging his foot out when any of them came too close. He dragged Dorothy over to the trough and let her go. Her head fell back into the mud, the pupils of her eyes large and unfocused. The pigs circled, the sow out in front.

Glazer looked down at Dorothy for a long moment, at the pool of dark blood forming in the middle of her abdomen. She coughed and blood bubbled up in her mouth. The sow surged forward a bit. Glazer turned and walked out of the pen.

The boy was crawling back to the house, leaving a wake of dirty blood in his passing. Glazer walked over to him and nudged him with a boot.

"Roll over," he said. "I want to get a look at you."

The boy slowly turned over and looked up. Glazer saw that the boy was older than he had thought, maybe fifteen or sixteen. Nearly a man.

"What's your name?" Glazer asked.

"Thomas," the boy said weakly. Blood slipped out of his mouth.

"My son's name was William, after my father. But you don't care much about that, do you?"

Thomas said nothing, his pupils wide with fear. Snot bubbled out of his nose and dripped onto his lips.

Glazer sat down onto his haunches and wiped the snot off of Thomas' face. "My son died when he was twelve years old. Wanted to be a doctor, or so he claimed. He was always talking about going to school in Kansas City. Hell of a thing, talking about heading off to school at his age, planning out his whole life. Seeing it all so clearly."

He ran the back of his hand gently down Thomas' face. "I'm awful sorry about this. I want you to know that. But some things can't be helped."

Glazer picked up Thomas and carried him toward the barn.

§

It took Harold nearly twenty minutes to return home.

Glazer sat inside of the house, on the far side of the kitchen table, his rifle aimed at the door, a gunnysack full of food at his feet. He heard Harold let out a series of whelping screams. Glazer couldn't tell who he had found first, but he guessed it was Thomas since he was clearly visible, strung up as he was just inside the barn. Glazer turned and tossed another log into the wood-burning stove. He positioned his Spencer so that it had a clean line of sight.

Moments later the door to the house burst open and Harold stumbled in. Glazer fired low, striking Harold in the left thigh. Harold toppled forward and collapsed just across the threshold of the house, his hands holding the gushing wound. Dust and gunpowder hung in the air. The fire in the stove cracked and popped. Glazer cocked the Spencer and got up and walked over and took away Harold's pistol.

"You'll have a limp, but you'll live." Glazer tossed the pistol back into the depths of the house.

Harold glared up at Glazer, his eyes narrow and dark. He tried to say something, but no words came out.

"I reckon you saw your boy."

"He was ... hanging all over the place!" Harold relaxed his grip on his thigh and blood spurted out of the bullet hole. Pain contorted his face and he put his hands back on the wound, squeezing down tight.

"It wasn't anything personal with poor Thomas. Wasn't his fault that he was born your son."

"W-what ... are you talking about?" Harold moved to stand up and Glazer lowered the rifle and aimed it at his head.

"Stay right there." Glazer turned and grabbed a chair and pulled it over to the door and sat directly in front of Harold. "You were one of Bloody Bill's boys. Running all over Missouri."

Harold's eyes were closed tight, his hands still wrapped around his leg wound. Blood trickled out between his fingers, coloring his hands a deep red.

Glazer pulled some chew out of his pocket and put a pinch into his mouth. He held the bag out to Harold. "Had to wait all damn morning for this. Want some?"

Harold shook his head, tears rolling down his face.

"Suit yourself." Glazer put the bag of chew back into his pocket. "You boys really tore it up outside of Fayette, didn't you? Found yourselves a nice little farm and thought you'd have some fun. Guess you were just warming up for what was to follow once you joined up with Bill."

"I ... I've never been to Missouri in my life."

"We both know that's a lie." Glazer raised the butt of the rifle and struck Harold directly in the forehead. Blood spilled from the wound and Harold went down, his eyes rolling back into his head. Glazer took him by the arms and dragged him out of the house, toward the barn. He left Harold there and walked back to the house.

Glazer tossed the gunnysack outside, then turned and picked up a large kerosene lantern that hung in the kitchen. He walked through the house, splashing the contents of the lantern on the floor, across the table and chairs, on a small desk, on the bed. He tossed the lantern into a corner and went for the stove.

He used an old pair of pincers to pull a burning log out of the stove and sent it across the floor, sparks and chunks of burning cinders spitting off as the wood rolled. The kerosene caught and burst into flames. After tossing another burning log onto one of the beds, Glazer turned and walked outside, grabbing the gunnysack as he went past it.

Harold lay sprawled out on the ground, his face covered with smeared blood. He looked like he wanted to scream, but no sound came out of his open mouth.

"Your wife's in with the pigs," Glazer said as he walked away.

§

Glazer's horse was hobbled in the middle of a cluster of pine trees about a mile from the Camp farm. He walked up to it, pulled down the saddlebag, and transferred the contents of the gunnysack. There was enough food for a week, maybe a little longer.

He folded up the gunnysack and pressed it down into the saddlebag. He opened a small flap on the front of the bag and took out a page from a newspaper. In the middle of the page was an ad featuring a long-haired woman. They could never afford a real picture and now this drawing was the only thing he had left. The smell of the fire drifted through the trees, the stink of burning wood and metal, and he breathed it in and he remembered her. Her face, her touch. Her lips. A fading apparition that grew thinner with each passing day, regardless of how much his heart ached. Regardless of anything.

Glazer put the ad back into the bag and untied his horse and led it out of the pine trees, toward a small path that ran perpendicular to the main road. He pulled himself up into the saddle and dug his heels into the horse's sides. It wouldn't be long before someone noticed the fire.

THURSDAY

1.

The two gravediggers were father and son. The son was short and fat and snorted through his nose, exhaling in large, meaty breaths. The father was thick and tall and wore a small black hat. Both were dressed in faded suits and the son's was too small for him, the buttons on the coat pushed to the breaking point. They carried the first casket out of the house, the father leading the way, and pushed it up onto the back of the wagon. The casket's wood was thin and nail heads jutted out of the seams along the top, where the lid was nailed down. A hard rain fell and the raindrops struck the wood with an empty thumping sound.

Harold Camp stood in the rain, looking at the box that held his son. Harold's head and leg were bandaged and he used a jagged piece of old wood as a crutch. His forehead was bruised and dark. Dorothy's aunt stood next to him, her face covered with a thin, black handkerchief held in place by a bonnet. She wore a faded black dress and clutched a framed picture of Dorothy to her chest. With her other hand, she held a tattered umbrella. The rest of the mourners stood in the rain, forming a line from the house to the wagon.

The gravediggers carried the second casket out of the house and they placed it on the back of the wagon and pushed it forward until only the very end of it dangled off the back of the wagon. After securing the caskets with thick straps, they walked to the front of the wagon and climbed up into the seat, the father taking the reins. The son wheezed under his breath and coughed lightly into his hand.

The wagon moved forward and the crowd fell behind it, Harold and the aunt leading the way. Harold limped as he walked, swinging the crutch through the mud the best he could.

The aunt's house was on the northern edge of Whitwell, and the road leading into town nothing more than brown water and dark mud. The wagon moved slowly, the horse taking care to maintain its traction in the slick mud.

A cluster of old buildings marked the edge of town, the wood exteriors faded and crumbling, windows gone, rooftops bowed from rot. Tall weeds grew everywhere. An old black man stood in the weeds near the edge of the road, a shovel in one hand. He watched the funeral procession go by, his eyes looking at each person following the wagon. Then he turned and vanished.

The road widened as it entered town. The buildings on either side of the road were made of brick or granite or wood, the shingles cobbled together from wood and slate, and on one of the structures pieces of old hide stretched over a hole in the roof and bounced in the rain. The front of what had been a barbershop was shot up from buckshot and rifle fire, the final evidence of a spate of violence that no one cared to remember.

The funeral procession moved through town. Off to one side of the road sat an abandoned wagon, its entire front axle gone, the wood bleached a cold white. Two old black men and a young black woman stood under an awning, watching the wagon pass. The woman was barefoot, her feet and ankles caked with mud. A white man appeared from inside the building and shooed them away, his arms waving in the air. With them gone, he turned and looked at the wagon for a moment. He shook his head and went back inside.

Lee Sinclair walked at the rear of the procession, his hat pulled low, the rain dribbling off of the rim. His boots cut through the mud and he moved slowly, so that he could stay well behind the main group. He knew people in town blamed him for what had happened to the Camps. Without him as sheriff, Whitwell was now a lawless town, and terrible things happened in such places. Or so people tended to believe, as if the mere act of having someone with a badge was enough to not only ward off evil but also the very nature of things. A small piece of stamped tin, the last bulwark against chaos. It made no sense, but Lee knew that there wasn't any reasoning with some folks.

On the day of the murders, Lee was one of the first people to reach the Camp farm. He'd seen the smoke, but by the time he got there, there was nothing to be done. The house was little more than smoldering ruins, the frames of the beds jutting up out of the blackened remains, the metal glowing a soft red. Camp was sprawled next to an old dogwood tree, muttering incomprehensibly about his son, his wife, his horse. When Lee went into the barn and saw Thomas hanging there, he nearly retched. He closed the doors to the barn and watched as Jesse Miller walked through the pig pen, shooting the pigs in the head, one by one. Such creatures couldn't be allowed to live.

The funeral procession neared the southern edge of town and a small group of people stood on the side of the road, watching them pass. Dorothy's aunt stumbled in the mud and the man behind her quickly reached forward and steadied her. The aunt burst into tears and the man quickened his pace and slipped an arm around her shoulders and she slumped against him, letting him carry most of her weight. Harold continued to walk next to her, staring at the caskets that carried his wife and child. His gaze did not deviate from the thin, unfinished wood that slowly stained and discolored from the constant rain.

The wagon pulled clear of Whitwell. The road narrowed and the father guided the wagon over to the side of the road, where the grass and weeds still held the earth together. The horse found the going easier and it raised its head, nostrils flaring as it caught its breath.

They headed up a hill to a small church and cemetery. Once the wagon cleared the gates, the procession broke off and moved toward the front of the church, where they waited for the preacher. The gravediggers continued on into the cemetery, following a thin trail to the northern edge of the grounds. They pulled the wagon to a stop near two open graves that were a tangle of mud and broken roots, that were filling with thick brown water. The father engaged the hand brake and they dropped down and started to undo the straps.

An old minister walked out of the church and into the rain. He wore a thick black slicker that was immediately soaked and his face was lined with sweat from the heat. A wide-brimmed hat sat on his head.

He walked over and shook Harold's free hand. He turned to the aunt and put his hands on her shoulders, bending close so that he could speak with her in private. After a moment, he released the aunt and without saying another word, he started toward the graves, the procession falling in behind him.

The minister walked around to the front of the open graves and Harold and the aunt took their places next to him. The rest of the mourners stood opposite them. Lee stood behind everyone else, not caring if he could see or not. He had lost count of how many men he had seen dumped into large, deep pits hollowed out of the earth, piled on top of each other, their limbs and blood mingling together until you couldn't tell where one man began and another ended. Adding a veneer of civilization, of God, didn't change anything. The ground didn't care either way.

The gravediggers looked at the minister and when he nodded they brought the caskets down from the wagon. They placed lines of rope under the first casket and lifted it, the son on one side of the grave and the father on the other. It dangled over the hole, the slick wood sliding a bit on the wet ropes, and they slowly lowered it, their hands straining to keep grip. The casket splashed as it landed at the bottom of the grave, waves of muddy water smacking against the thin wood.

"My friends," the minister said, his arms raised up, the rain running off of the sleeves of his coat. "We are here to pay our final respects to Dorothy and Thomas Camp. Their lives were stolen from them — and from us — in the most heinous of circumstances."

The gravediggers started to lower the second casket down into the ground. Sweat ran down their faces and their armpits were dark from the effort. The son wheezed. Heat hung in the air like a thick, suffocating blanket. The minister nodded as the second coffin came to rest.

"Murder is a terrible sin," the minister said. "It is the opposite of God. It defiles everything that God stands for. And what we see before us is but the latest in a long line of affronts to our people, to our values. The assault continues day and night, and we are forced to watch, to accept what is being done to us."

There was a murmuring of amens among the people gathered. Lee moved to the side and pulled his wet shirt away from his skin. A couple of people standing near him glanced in his direction, but when he met their eyes, they looked away.

"But we will not be cowed, and we will not be defeated," the minister continued. "For come the day of the final judgment, all of those that seek to destroy us, all of those that have committed physical and spiritual murder upon us, shall be forced to answer for their crimes. And God will strip them down to nothing, and they will face him in their shame and when he asks why they have done such things, they will have no answer. For they have no claim to righteousness, no claim to God at all. Their lies will at last be exposed and God will cast them down into the pit where they shall suffer and toil with their wicked brothers and sisters for all of eternity."

One of the gravediggers took a shovel and began to fill in the hole. Harold winced as the thick, muddy earth struck the casket's thin wood. The water at the bottom of the hole eddied as the weight of the dirt forced the casket down. Dorothy's aunt began to openly weep and she turned away, unable to watch.

"We all stand here in the heat and the muck and the filth, and we see the grief on faces of Thomas and Dorothy's family," said the minister. "And we ask ourselves, what can I take from this? What lesson is there to learn? And I tell you the lesson is simple. Do not turn your back on God. Do not ignore him. Observe the Sabbath. Remember to tithe. For the man who abandons God abandons God's protection, and that man is alone in the dark of the wilderness. Evil shall seek him out. But if we stay true and righteous to our God, to our families and yes, to our proud heritage, then we shall be saved." The minister extended his hands forward, toward the graves, the rain rolling off his black coat.

"I pray that we all take solace in the knowledge that Dorothy and Thomas were baptized before the Lord and that their souls were free of sin when they died. For that is the promise Jesus Christ made to us on the cross. And though our hearts ache at their passing, know that they are in a better place, a place free from pain and suffering. Do not dwell on the pain you feel at their loss, but instead revel in the joy that they brought to us when they were alive. Lord Jesus, we pray in your name. Amen."

Dorothy's aunt was uncontrollable in her grief. The minister motioned for two men and they walked over and took her by the arms and started for the church. The minister patted Harold on the shoulder and followed the aunt.

Harold looked down at the two holes in the ground. Rivulets of rain streamed down his face and caught in his beard. He raised a hand and wiped his eyes clear. Thunder rumbled overhead and he looked up at the sky as if it held the answer to his grief. Harold lowered his head and pinched his eyes shut with two fingers.

The gravediggers now shoveled in earnest, scooping up big clumps of heavy, wet earth and dumping them into each hole. The air echoed with the sound of hollow thumping as the clay and dirt struck the lids of the caskets. Harold turned and walked away, the wooden crutch slipping and sliding in the mud as he walked. A man reached out and took him by the arm and helped him back toward the church.

Lee watched the gravediggers work. The graves filled quickly and soon the only sound was that of dark earth striking dark earth. The top of one of the graves eroded away and water began to pour in. The gravediggers ignored it and kept shoveling.

Only a few people remained in the cemetery and most of them were visiting the graves of loved ones. An old man knelt next to a small headstone, one hand resting on top of it. He was saying something, but Lee couldn't hear what it was. Probably telling whoever was buried there that he still loved them, that he missed them. Lots of people spoke to the dead. Sometimes it was the only way to get past the grief.

Lee walked across the cemetery to a thin, granite headstone. The name on it was Gertrude Pierce, and he knelt down and ran a hand across the headstone's wet face. His sister had died of pneumonia while he was away and it was getting harder for him to remember what she looked like. Her voice was already long forgotten, erased so thoroughly from his memory that sometimes it seemed as if he had never heard her speak. He feared the day when her face disappeared as well.

He stood up and wiped the rain from his eyes and walked back toward the road. As he went by the church, he nodded to a couple of men sitting on the steps. One of them was missing his right arm, the sleeve neatly pinned up under his armpit. They both tipped their hats as Lee walked out onto the road and headed back for town, alone.

On the edge of town, Lee turned east and followed a smaller road for about a quarter of a mile until he reached a narrow shack and a large barn. Behind the shack were four stacks of sacked feed, a net tied over the top of them and a loose tarp on top of that. Two cats sat under the tarp, watching him.

The inside of the shack was small and hot and dark. Shovels and rakes leaned against one wall, the handles dusty, the blades covered with dried dirt. Scattered around the implements were old gunnysacks and bags, most folded in half, left to sit on the floor. A small wood counter ran along the back wall, and behind it was a doorway that was covered with a dirty sheet. Another cat slept on the counter, rolled up in a ball.

Lee slapped the water off of his hat and walked over to the counter. He ran a hand down the cat's back and it softly purred, not moving. Lee knocked on the counter. "Paul, you back there?"

From the back room came a sound and a moment later a tall, thin man appeared. He pulled his suspenders over his bare chest and wiped the sleep from his eyes.

"Odd time of the day to be sleeping," Lee said.

"Was up most of the night dealing with a sick heifer," Paul said.

"Save it?"

"No." Paul sat down on a stool and cleared his throat. He spit out a thick wad of brown muck and put in a chew. The cat walked over to Paul and flopped down in front of him. "I tell you, something is going around. That's the third one this week."

"Never seems to end, does it?"

"Nope." Paul spit out a wad of tobacco and rubbed the cat's belly. The cat purred and slid around on its back.

"I hate asking you, but you wouldn't happen to have that money you owe me, would you?"

"If I had it, woulda brought it out to you."

"It's been nearly two months, Paul."

"I know how long it's been. But I can't pay what I don't have. Hell,

26

half the people in this town owe me money, and not a one of them has a dollar to their name. Until they pay me, there's nothing I can do."

"Christ."

"Can't even haggle anything worth a damn out of most folks. They beg me for feed, say if their stock dies, I'll never get paid. Drag my ass out all hours of night, want me to look at a cow that's got the scours. What the hell choice do I have? Damn thing shits all over me then falls over dead." Paul spit. "I come back from the war to this two-bit shack and not much else. Shit, I'm surprised it hasn't fallen over."

"I was lucky I got to keep my horse."

"Fucking country. I should've joined up with the federal army. At least I'd have some money to my name."

"You really think they would've taken you?"

"From what I hear, they'd take about anyone as long as you didn't have any issues with shooting Indians." The cat stood up, butted its head against Paul's arm. It jumped off the counter and disappeared into the back room. "You go to the funeral?"

"It's where I was coming from."

"You went out to the farm, right? After it happened?"

"Yeah."

"Glad I didn't have to see that. Missus all torn up from the pigs, his son. Well, you were there. Don't need me beatin' on it. Many people show up?"

"Twenty, maybe thirty. I think the rain kept folks away."

"Camp say anything to you?"

"Didn't even look at me."

"I ever tell you that I went out there one time to help that sow of his have her litter? Couple of them got turned around up inside of her, and she couldn't get them out. Had to reach all the way up there and drag them out and all the while that sow is kicking and snorting like she was possessed by the Devil himself. That bitch almost bit my hand off. What a fucking mess." Paul spit, the brown saliva striking the stained floor behind the counter.

"Anyway, I was waiting around to get paid, and Camp lays into that wife of his over some thing or another, she didn't get enough firewood or something. I thought he was going to beat her to death. Then he comes over to me, huffing and puffing and asking what the hell I was waiting around for, and I stand my ground and tell him that he has to pay me, that I don't stick my hands up inside of a pig for the fun of it. His face is all red, his hands shaking, and I'm thinking about how fast I can get the knife out of my boot.

Then he storms into the house and comes back out and pays me and tells me to get the hell off his property. Fucking prick. If someone was going to get fed to those pigs, it should've been him."

"I heard some stories about him from the war, how he'd kill women and children, any man who made the mistake of getting in his way. Never could tell what was true, though."

"Based on what I saw, I'd believe every word of it."

"Listen, I need to get over to the shop. Any chance you might get some money this week?"

"You'll be the first to know."

"I can't keep going on like this. I'm a month behind on the rent the way it is."

"None of us can. But what's to be done about it?"

"Hell if I know." Lee turned away from the counter and started toward the door.

"Listen," Paul said. "I'll come out to your place in a couple days, help you around the shop." He stood up and walked around the counter. "Ain't going to be as good as money, but maybe we can turn some jobs around, try and get things moving."

"I appreciate that. Sorry I woke you up."

"Tell the missus hello for me."

"I will." Lee stepped outside and walked back toward town. The sky was clearing, and the sun came down in sharp bursts between the passing clouds. Lee followed the lane, his boots slapping in the mud as he walked.

2.

Glazer screwed the woman from behind, her skirts pushed up around her waist, her head down and buried in the pillow. He'd told the whore not to look up, not to make a sound. He looked at the small of her back, the beads of sweat pooling there, and conjured up the picture from the advertisement, trying to remember how she smelled, the sounds she made when they loved. He focused on the whore's ass, how the flesh slapped when he thrust in her. It could be anyone's ass. It had to be.

He finished with a grunt and some small thrusts. He pulled out and pushed himself off the back of the bed. He stood there, naked and stiff. The whore was still face down, not moving, unsure if he was really done.

"You can go now," Glazer said.

The whore stood up and pushed down her skirts, wiped the sweat from her face. "Was it good?"

"It was fine."

"You want me to give you a bath? I know how to shave."

"I said you can go."

The whore looked at him for a moment, straightened her skirts. She turned and walked out the door, closing it quickly behind her. Glazer stood there, looking at the room. A bed, peeling wallpaper, a bureau with an old mirror. Two dusty windows. The floor was rough, made of uneven wood. How many men had passed through here?

Glazer turned and looked at himself in the bureau's mirror. There were dark circles under his eyes and his hair was thinning and unkempt. Dirt and dried sweat stained his chest, and filth was packed into the wrinkles in his neck, creating thin black lines that ran under his jaw. A ring of deep scars crossed his chest from where the grapeshot had struck him, the skin mottled a faint gray. The scar on his forehead was pale, lighter than the rest of his face. He stared at the scars and tried to remember the pain of their creation, but could not. So much of him had faded away to nothingness and there, naked in front of the mirror, he finally welcomed it. There was no point in holding on to things that were already gone.

Glazer turned away from the mirror and got dressed.

§

The bar downstairs was nearly empty, just a couple of men sitting in a corner, playing a card game of some kind. Neither was drinking anything.

Glazer came down the stairs, his saddlebag in one hand, and walked over to the bar. He motioned for the bartender, a short, bald man dressed in a fraying suit and a small red tie.

"What'll you have," the bartender asked.

"Whiskey."

"Don't have any bourbon. All I got is straight corn."

"That's fine with me."

"All right, then."

Glazer looked around the bar and saw the whore over in a corner, talking to another woman. The whore was motioning to the woman, showing her how she had to keep her head down, how he didn't want to see her face. Glazer looked away.

The bartender placed the shot of whiskey on the bar and Glazer sipped it, letting it burn down his throat.

"You want another?"

"No, just the one," Glazer said. He finished the shot and placed the empty glass down onto the bar.

"Should I settle your bill?"

"That'd be fine."

"Looks like it'll be four dollars and twenty cents."

Glazer reached into a front pocket and pulled out a small wad of bills and peeled off five dollars and placed it on the counter. As he waited for his change, he looked at the bartender.

"You happen to know a man by the name of Harlan Prescott?"

"I might," the bartender said as he handed Glazer his change. "What's your business with him?"

"Fought with him during the war, over in the Carolinas. Remember he said he was from these parts. Thought I'd pay him a visit."

"I took you for a Yankee."

"I come out of Missouri." Glazer turned serious. "Southern Missouri."

The bartender's face relaxed. "Harlan lives just south of town, not more than ten miles. House is off the road a bit, near some willow trees."

"He live out there with his family?"

"Not anymore. Yellow fever took his wife and daughter. Must've been eight months ago. Maybe nine. He's all alone now."

Glazer shook his head. "I'm sorry to hear that."

"Nothing worse than losing your family. It'll tear a man's guts out."

"Ain't that the truth." Glazer collected his belongings and walked away from the bar.

"I'm sure Harlan will be glad to see a friendly face."

Glazer nodded and stepped outside. He turned left and walked along the front of the building before turning into a small alley where his horse was tied. After securing his bag, he let the horse loose and led it out to the road.

§

The Prescott farm was set back from the road, at the end of an L-shaped lane. A row of large willow trees ringed the southern side of the property, near the rear of the house. On the other side of the lane was a small shed and a barn. The house was in disrepair, but the barn looked brand-new, as if it had been built in the last year. Glazer sat in a stand of trees across the road, watching. He'd been there for an hour and all was quiet.

Glazer turned and looked back toward town. He didn't know how often people used this road. It was narrow and a long strip of wild grass grew down its middle. On either side of the grass were deep troughs, dug into the earth by the weight of each passing wagon. He looked back toward town again. There was nothing. He looked at the sky, squinted at the sun. It was late afternoon. Glazer picked up his Spencer and walked across the road, cutting to the north, toward a row of thin oaks. When he reached them, he dropped down onto his haunches. He could just make out the front door of the house and Glazer sat there for a few minutes, waiting to see if anyone had heard his approach. Satisfied that no one had, he moved in a semicircle around the farm, keeping out of sight of the door, his eyes watching for any movement. The only sound was the crowing of a rooster. Glazer knelt next to the shed and checked the rifle. He got up and walked toward the front door of the house. He lowered the rifle so that it was flush with his right leg and knocked on the door.

"Who is it?" The man's voice came from the depths of the house.

"You Harlan Prescott?"

Boots shuffled across hardwood, and a moment later Harlan Prescott stood in the doorway. He was shirtless, his belly hanging over the top of his filthy pants. His eyes were bloodshot and he stunk of whiskey. "Who the hell are you?"

"I'm looking for Harlan Prescott."

31

"You found him."

"Harlan Prescott who fought in Missouri?"

"What business is that of yours?"

Glazer raised the rifle and aimed it at Harlan's face. "Did you fight in Missouri?"

"I was up in Missouri for a while, yeah. Did some guerrilla work before I came back down and joined up proper." Harlan's eyes moved from the rifle to Glazer and back. "You aiming to rob me? I ain't got a damn thing to my name." He gestured toward the inside of the house. "Hell, take a look."

"Come on out of there." Glazer backed away from the door, the rifle still aimed at Harlan.

Harlan slowly stepped out of the house, his hands fidgeting at his sides. Slobber dripped from his bottom lip and he wiped it away.

"Turn around," Glazer said. "In a slow circle."

After looking at the Spencer again, Harlan turned until he once again faced Glazer.

"You got anything in those boots?" Glazer asked.

"Just my feet." He lost his balance for a moment and took a step forward, barely righting himself.

Glazer motioned with the rifle. "What's back there, past the trees?"

"Nothing. A field. After a ways it turns into swamp."

"How far back does the swamp go?"

"All the way to the river."

"Then that's where we're going. Put your hands on the top of your head and start walking. You make one move and you're dead."

"What the hell's this about? I ain't never done anything to you." Harlan's eyes were now wide with fear. "I already told you I don't have nothing worth stealing."

"Just walk."

He turned and started east, toward the swamp, his hands on the top of his head. Beads of sweat rolled down his back and a sour whiskey smell floated in his wake. Glazer followed, the rifle aimed square at the back of Harlan's head. They walked past the barn, an old wagon, and a large pile of wood. Beyond the woodpile, the land sloped down and leveled out as it turned into an unkempt field, weeds and shattercane growing everywhere.

"I understand your family is dead," Glazer said.

"That's right." Harlan's voice was dry, cracked. He coughed lightly in an effort to clear his throat. "Lost both of them within a couple of days."

"Where are they buried?"

"What's that got to do with anything?"

"Answer me."

"They're buried in town, in the cemetery." He glanced back at Glazer. "What the hell do you want?"

"Is it a family plot?"

"You're not making any sense, mister." Harlan shook from fear and anger. Glazer pressed the end of the Spencer against the back of his skull. "Yes, it's a family plot. Three generations of my kin is buried there."

"That's what I thought."

The two men walked across the field, their boots slopping through the mud and standing water. On the far side of the field, the land rose a bit before it dropped back down. Past the natural levee was the swamp, the water brown and stagnant, old trees rising up from the muck, dark moss growing on the trunks. Harlan reached the edge of the water and stopped.

"I didn't say to stop," Glazer said.

Harlan turned around. His eyes were full of fear, his tongue endlessly licking his lips. "There's no call for this. Please, mister, I'm begging you. I can't swim."

"It's either the swamp or a bullet. You decide."

Harlan started forward, his boots sloshing through the dark water, his legs fighting to keep their balance. The water quickly deepened to his thighs. He panted heavily, taking in big gulping breaths as he struggled through the water, his hands out for balance. Glazer followed him.

"Tell me about what you did up in Missouri," Glazer said as they walked.

"Hell, I don't know. Raided some towns, killed some Yanks. Same as everyone else."

"Same as everyone else."

"That's right." He stumbled and barely caught his balance. Water splashed all over him. "My boots are full of water."

"Head for that big tree over there," Glazer said.

Harlan sloshed his way toward a tall, thick tree. Its dark trunk was surrounded by a bramble of weeds and dead logs and other pieces of flotsam. The water was nearly pitch black and stunk of drowned rot. Insects buzzed through the air and a chorus of toads croaked in the distance.

He reached the tree and stopped, one hand on its trunk. He panted, fighting to catch his breath, his back to Glazer. His entire body dripped with sweat.

"Turn around," Glazer said. Harlan stumbled as he turned and nearly fell again and had to use the tree to right himself. Dirty water ran down his belly.

"I'll ask you again — what did you do in Missouri?"

"I didn't do nothing! Jesus, please. What do you want!"

"There was a farm near Fayette. You know what I'm talking about."

Recognition flashed across Harlan's face. "Oh Lord."

"When your wife died, how long did she suffer?"

"Jesus almighty. Listen to me, you have my word. I didn't have nothing to do with that."

"I hear that yellow fever is a horrible way to die what with all of the bleeding and vomiting. Must've been a terrible sight. Lots of screaming, I'd imagine. Heartbreaking to watch."

"I didn't know, they just told me to keep watch. You have to believe me."

"How long did it take your wife to die?"

"I'll give you the farm. Anything. I didn't lay a hand on either of them!"

"Answer me!"

Tears ran down Harlan's face and his breathing was shallow and thick. He kept a hand on the tree, fingers digging into the bark. Pieces of it broke off and slowly fell to the water below. "Three days, maybe four. I don't remember exactly."

"What about your girl?"

"She died fast, in her sleep." He wiped the tears away from his face. "Thank Christ for that."

"Did it break your heart seeing them die?"

"Of course it did." Harlan's voice turned into a whisper. "Of course it did."

"Those kinds of wounds don't ever heal. They just grow and grow, until the rot has consumed every part of you. And by the time you realize the scope of it, it's too late. At that point, there's no going back."

"Why won't you believe me?"

"No one's going to find your body. Not out here in this bog. That plot in the cemetery, next to your wife and child? It'll always be empty."

"Please ... I've lost everything. I ask you as a Christian to show me mercy."

"I'm about as far from Christian as you can get." Glazer shot Harlan in the face. The sound of the shot echoed through the swamp and Harlan's knees gave out and he fell straight down, landing with a loud splash in the dark water. His body floated in the muck, blood spooling away from the wound in his face. Glazer walked over to the corpse and nudged it toward the bramble and grabbed some of the dead limbs and piled them over the top of the body, their weight pushing it down, below the surface of the water. Glazer stood and looked down, waiting for the water to calm. There was a small flurry of air bubbles. After a few moments, nothing of the man was visible.

Satisfied, Glazer turned and headed for shore. When he was clear of the swamp, he pulled off his boots, dumped out the water, and walked back toward the Prescott farm, the boots hanging from one hand. The sun was much lower now. It'd be completely dark in a couple of hours.

When Glazer reached the house, he placed his boots upside down by the steps and pulled off his socks and went inside. The main room was large and dark, a stained and wretched bed pushed against one wall. Next to the bed was a small table, which was covered with empty whiskey bottles. Glazer walked over to the bed and used the tip of the rifle barrel to sort through a stack of dirty clothes piled at the end of the mattress.

Not finding anything of interest, Glazer went into the kitchen. A small wood-burning stove sat in the center of the room, the top and front of it slick from old grease. Stacked in one corner, inside of a vegetable crate, were a dozen sealed canning jars. Some were marked with a circle, some with an X to mark they might be suspect. Otherwise the kitchen was empty.

Glazer went into the pantry, which was piled high with all manner of clothing. He pushed through it with the rifle and pulled out two dresses, a pair of shoes that a little girl might wear. Under some muddy overalls he found three socks. He knelt and picked them up and separated them. One of them had a hole, so he set it aside, but the other two were still in one piece. Glazer put the rifle on the floor and sat down and pulled on the socks. They stunk of old sweat, but they were dry. Glazer picked up his rifle and one of the dresses and walked back to the front door.

Once back outside, he sat on the step, and used the dress to dry the inside of his boots. When he was satisfied he tossed aside the dress and pulled the small piece of paper and lead from his breast pocket. He carefully unfolded it and crossed Harlan Prescott's name off the list.

Four names remained.

3.

Lee plunged the horseshoe into a trough of dirty water, the water spitting and hissing from the hot metal. He held it underwater for a couple of minutes. Once he was certain the metal had set, he pulled it out of the water and tossed it onto a pile of shoes that sat on a bare patch of dead earth.

The blacksmith shop was old and decrepit — a single, large room with a forge, a pile of coal and wood, and assorted metal-working tools that hung from the walls. The ground was barren and in some places scorched black where fires had broken out. Lee took a drink from a small canteen and picked up the bellows and fanned up the flames.

With the horseshoes done, all he had left to do was repair a wagon wheel. The forge was small, so he was going to have to work it slowly, bit by bit, heating it up a section at a time. It was going to be a slow and tedious job, but there was no way around it. He couldn't afford to upgrade any of the equipment.

Lee pulled on a pair of old, burned leather gloves, the hide around the tips of the fingers scorched and peeling, and lifted the wheel and placed it on the edge of the forge. Sweat ran down his face and arms.

"Lee," a man's voice said. Lee turned and looked toward the doorway. Three men stood there. He didn't recognize two of them, but the third one was Oliver Hansford.

"What do you want?" Lee asked.

"Just a few moments of your time," Hansford said. Despite the overpowering heat and thick, moist air, Hansford was dressed in his Sunday best, white pants and jacket, his mustache clinging to his chubby face. The two men with Hansford were stocky, built low, wide across the chest. One of them wore a bandanna across the bottom of his face, covering everything but his eyes. "May we speak outside? It's dreadfully hot in here."

"Make it quick, I've got work to do." Lee dropped the wheel to the ground, disengaged the bellows, and walked toward the front of the shop.

Hansford and the other two men followed Lee. The front of the shop was a jumble of old plows and metal parts and broken-down wagons. Off to one side was a pile of scrap metal. The town's livery was across the street and the smell of horse manure hung in the air. Hansford's carriage sat on the side of the road, a black man in the front. He wore a simple black suit and stared ahead at nothing. Two horses were tied to the back of the carriage.

"Let's hear it," Lee said. He pulled off his gloves and ran a hand through his sweat-slickened hair.

"I wish to discuss the horrible atrocities that were inflicted upon poor Harold Camp," Hansford said. "And what's being done to bring the perpetrator to justice."

"I hope you didn't come here thinking I was going to get wrapped up in all of that. It's not my concern. Not anymore."

"On the contrary, I feel it is."

"I'm not the sheriff. Haven't been since the war. You know that."

"You're the only person in town qualified to hold the position. I'd hoped that once enough time passed, you'd come to your senses and recognize your true place here."

"This town is crawling with ex-soldiers looking for work. Any of them would be more than happy to take over." Lee turned and started back toward the shop. "I've got work to do."

"You were a hero during the war, Lee. A true son of the Confederacy. And that's why it breaks my heart to watch you turn yellow."

Lee stopped and turned back to Hansford. "Easy words coming from a man who didn't lift a damned finger during the war."

"I did my part. I assure you."

"From where? That big old ranch in Texas?"

"Not all fighting's done with a gun."

Lee laughed. "I bet it was rough out there, sitting around, sipping your sweet tea. Probably didn't have to worry too much about getting shot at, did you? Or where your next meal was coming from."

"Did you know that the man who butchered Harold's family is a Yankee? Harold told me himself, said he could tell by his accent. The war isn't over, Lee. It'll never be over. That's why we need to do whatever is necessary to protect our own. We need law and order. We need to show the Yankees that they are not free to ride roughshod through our lands, doing what they please. We need to show the people of this town that they are safe from northern tyranny and are free to live their lives as they choose."

"Get the hell out of here." Lee looked at Hansford and motioned with an arm. "Go on, get."

"This is my property, Lee. I have every right to stand here as long as I wish."

"Like hell it is. This land belongs to old man Guthrie. My lease is with him."

"Not anymore, it isn't." Hansford opened up his coat and pulled a yellow envelope from an inside pocket. He removed a piece of paper and held it out to Lee. "Go on, read it."

Lee walked over and took the paper, unfolded it, and started to read.

"It's quite simple," Hansford said. "Earlier today I visited Mr. Guthrie and made him a fair offer on this property. That's the bill of sale, which means that you are now my tenant."

"What the hell do you want with me?" Lee said. He folded the paper back up.

"Starting tomorrow morning, you will once again be the sheriff of this town. Should you refuse, I will evict you for being one month past due on rent and seize everything on the premises. I'm sure you've heard that the government plans on levying higher taxes in order to rebuild the railroad. Without this shop, how will you pay those taxes when they come due? And when you don't pay them, the government will seize that scrap of property you own and that will be the end of it. You'll be left with nothing."

"You're a son of a bitch."

"Perhaps. But I am also a man of my word, and I have no qualms in doing whatever's needed to bring order back to this county. Tomorrow morning, you and my two associates will set off after the murderer. You will not return until he's either captured or confirmed dead. In the latter instance, you will return his body to me."

"I'm not leaving my family, Hansford. Not again."

"You have my word that they'll be safe. I shall even pay them your salary, from my own pocket."

Lee fingered his wedding ring.

"Men need to know their place in the world," Hansford said. He took the paper back from Lee and walked toward his carriage, the two other men following. "You leave at dawn."

Lee watched the two men untie the horses. Hansford climbed into the back of the carriage, removed his hat, and knocked on the side. The black man worked the reigns and the carriage started forward, the two men following. Lee stood there and watched them, clenching and unclenching his hands.

§

Lee walked down the road toward his land, sixteen acres about four miles north of Whitwell. The house was set off from the main road and connected via a circular lane. Across from the house was a small shed, a corral for a horse, and a chicken pen. The remains of an old barn sat crumbling in a field, the collapsed, rotting wood covered in tall weeds and grass. Behind the house was a small grove of pine trees and a garden.

The property had been in Lee's family for two generations, and he had inherited it after his father passed away. At the time, the house was in excellent condition, freshly painted with new windows. During the war, it slowly fell into a state of disrepair. The paint cracked and peeled, shingles coming loose, and the window frames warped and bent from the relentless humidity. It had been too much for his wife Kate to manage, especially given that wood was so hard to come by. Every scrap was seized by the Confederate government and shipped off so that it could be turned into wagons, railroad ties, or whatever else they could think of.

Lee turned off the road and went to the back door. He scraped the mud off the bottom of his boots and went inside. The house smelled of fried potatoes and onions and liver.

He went into the kitchen and sat down at the table. Kate Sinclair stood next to the kitchen table, an old cast iron skillet in one hand.

"You're late," she said. Her hair was pulled back into a bun and her face was streaked with sweat, but even through the kitchen grime she was quite beautiful, her sharp features complementing her soft eyes.

"Damn it's hot in here. That window open?" Lee shifted his chair a bit, trying to get it away from the part of the floor that sloped to the south. Someday he was going to have to get some chunks of granite and patch up that foundation.

"As far as it'll go. Grab a plate and get something to eat before it gets cold." Kate placed the skillet on a towel in the middle of the table and went back to the stove. "Where were you?"

"After the funeral I had to take care of some things, and I decided to finish up with that wheel." Lee poured himself a glass of sun tea from a pitcher and took a long drink. He put the glass down and spooned a helping of food out of the skillet and onto his plate.

"Thought it wasn't due for another couple of days?" Kate said.

Lee took a bite of the food. The potatoes weren't cooked all the way through, but he didn't say anything. Instead he smashed them flat and mixed them with the onions and took another bite. "Wanted to get it done. Where's Jeremiah?" Nearly three years had been cut away from father and son while Lee was fighting in the war, and now he was going to leave again. Thinking about it made his chest hot with anger.

"In his room. I didn't know when you were getting home, so I went ahead and let him eat."

Lee took another bite of food. "Hansford came by the shop today. Started up with that business about me being sheriff."

"I don't care what that man says, you're done with that work."

"It's not that simple."

"Why not? He doesn't have the right to tell you what to do." Kate sat down at the table and took a drink of her coffee.

"If I don't track down the man who killed Camp's family, Hansford will take the shop."

"He doesn't own that property."

"He bought it from Guthrie this morning."

Kate slammed her coffee cup down onto the table. "I don't believe this. Why would he sell it? That land's been in his family for a hundred years."

"Because he's broke, same as everyone else." Lee took another bite of his food. "And you heard what Emory said about property taxes. Just because we own this land doesn't mean the government can't take it."

"We need to talk to Guthrie, get him to cancel the sale."

"He's not going to do that. Once he got the money from Hansford that was the end of it."

"You can't do this, Lee. I won't be able to stomach it."

"I don't have any choice."

"There has to be a way out of this," Kate said. Tears formed in her eyes and one of them slid down her face. "There are people in this town that will back you up, take your side."

"No one around here is going to stand up to Hansford. They can't afford to cross him."

"I waited here for three years, night and day, worrying myself sick over whether you were going to come home missing an arm or a leg, or come home at all. And when you walked through that door without so much as a scratch on you, that was the end of it. No more guns, no more being gone for days and weeks at a time. None of that."

"I know."

"You gave me your word, Lee. The day you came home, I made you swear to me."

"I don't do this, we lose everything."

"That's better than losing my husband, than Jeremiah losing his father. We'll find something else."

"There isn't anything else, Kate. This is it."

"We'll sell our land, move up north, get away from here."

Lee pushed his plate away and looked at his wife. "Who in the hell is going to buy this land? I can't even get the money I'm owed on a three-dollar axle repair!"

"Don't yell at me."

Lee looked at the table for a moment. He lifted his head, looked at his wife. "There's no way out of this. Believe me, I thought about it on the way home."

"What happens after? He just lets you go back to blacksmithing?"

"Doubt it."

"I knew this would all come back around on us. It was only a matter of time." Kate stood and walked over to the counter and put her head down, crying. He went to her, wrapping his arms around her.

"I won't be gone long," Lee said. "I promise. I'll do this one thing, then we'll figure out where to go from there. Set a little aside, think about moving once we're ahead."

"You did your part!" Kate turned and faced Lee. Tears ran down her face. "Why can't those cowards let you alone?"

Lee pulled his wife tight. There was nothing else to say.

§

Jeremiah was stretched out on his bed, a small book open in front of him. Lee walked into the room and sat down in the small wooden chair next to the bed. Lee's father had made it for Jeremiah a couple of months before he died, and Jeremiah insisted on keeping it in his room, close to his bed.

"What are you working on?" Lee asked.

"Just reading."

"Is that what your mother asked you to do?"

"No, sir. I'm all finished with her lessons." Once it became clear that the war was going to last longer than anyone had thought it was going to, most of the schools closed, the women too busy to teach. Kate, however, had taken an armful of books from an abandoned schoolhouse and insisted on teaching Jeremiah herself. War or not, there was no reason to be ignorant, she said. She started when Jeremiah was six, and here he was, a little past nine. How the years went on by. A man could blink and miss his entire life.

"I wanted to tell you that I have to go away in the morning. Maybe for a month or more."

Jeremiah sat up and looked at Lee. "You said you weren't going to leave again."

"I know what I said, but this is something I have to do."

"What about Momma?" Jeremiah looked his father and his eyes grew wide.

"You'll have to watch out for her. Help her around the house, pick up some extra chores. I have a few things down at the shop that need to be delivered. Your mother has a list. You'll see to them?"

"Yes, sir."

Lee leaned back in the chair and breathed in the room. It smelled of pencil lead and paper and soap. Jeremiah had always been a meticulous boy, one who had to keep things in their proper place, never leaving anything to chance.

"Where you going?" Jeremiah asked.

"My guess is down to Georgia. Maybe over to South Carolina."

"Why?"

"Have to see about a man."

"A criminal?"

"That's right."

"Is he dangerous?"

"They're all dangerous."

"Momma is going to be upset."

"She already is."

"What happens when you get back?"

"How do you mean?"

"Are you going to be sheriff again?"

"I don't know. It depends, I guess."

"On what?"

"On what happens when I get back."

"What if you get shot?"

"I won't get shot."

"How do you know?"

"I didn't live through three years of war to get shot by some idiot. I'll be fine."

"I don't want you to leave."

"Neither do I. But sometimes life forces you to do things you don't want to do and there's nothing you can do about it."

"Who's going to run the shop?"

"Any job that isn't done is going to have to wait."

"I can keep it clean. Make sure no birds or rats get in there. You know how they like to nest."

Lee looked at his son. "You do what your mother says. I'll be back before you know it." He stood and walked out of the room, slowly closing the door behind him.

4.

Glazer rode through the night, the soft light of the full moon illuminating the land around him in washed grays and blacks. The moon was so bright that some of the oak trees lining the road cast shadows. His horse moved at a good clip, following the road.

He had crossed into Georgia earlier in the day and once he was a few miles across the state line, Glazer climbed a small hill that overlooked the road and he hobbled his horse. He wanted to see who else was using the road, but after a couple of hours, the only people who had passed by were two black men, an old mule lugging their belongings. As soon as it was dark, Glazer continued on.

The road widened a bit as it approached an old wooden bridge that stretched across a creek. Glazer pulled his horse to a stop and looked for an approach down to the water. After a moment he spotted a deer trail. He nudged his horse toward the trail and went down. When they reached the creek, Glazer climbed off the horse, which lowered its head and started to drink.

Glazer pulled a small piece of cloth out of his saddlebag and walked over to the creek and dipped it in the cold water. He ran it across his forehead and eyes, wiping away the dried sweat and dirt that covered his skin. He soaked the cloth again and wiped down his throat and his arms. The creek was narrow and shallow and toads croaked in the darkness. Glazer bent over, putting his face in the water. He took a drink, the cold water rushing down his throat. He kept his face in the water for a few moments then he raised his head and shook his face dry.

The horse backed away from the water and sneezed twice, blowing water out of its nose. Glazer checked its face. Damn thing drank too fast, he thought. He took it by the reins and led it back up onto the road.

He walked with the horse for a while, giving it time to work through the water. The last thing he needed was it getting sick.

The road narrowed again and the trees fell away. Glazer climbed back up into the saddle and the horse started forward at a light trot, the sound of its hooves echoing in the night air.

The road continued on straight for ten miles before it curved and widened. As Glazer came around the curve, he saw the darkened shadow of a ruined house about a quarter mile up the road. He steered his horse off the road and approached at a wide angle, watching the house all the while, looking for any sign of fire or movement. All was dark and quiet. Glazer gently moved the horse toward the house.

The house was two stories tall, and the wall on the east side had partially collapsed, opening a large hole in the side. The roof over the hole sagged, the remaining wooden supports barely keeping the slates and shingles in place. The ground beneath the hole was littered with wood and plaster and shingles. A front porch ran the width of the house.

Glazer stopped the horse a few feet from the front door and dismounted. He slowly walked around the side of the house, one hand leading the horse by the reins. The yard was overrun with weeds, and Glazer saw the shadowed forms of old furniture and rusted farm equipment. The sounds of toads and crickets filled the air. He stopped next to a couch and pushed it with one foot. The cushions were soft and saturated with moisture and rot. One hard blow and the whole thing would fall apart.

Glazer looked past the debris field, toward the back of the property. A smashed cotton gin sat on top of a wooden platform. Beyond that was a thick grove of cypress trees and beyond the trees was nothing but black.

He turned and looked at the back of the house. The area near the back door was charred black from fire, but someone had managed to extinguish it before it had spread out of control. All of the windows were gone.

Glazer tied his horse to an old rusted plow and walked toward the back door. The inside of the house was dark, and he moved carefully, using his boots to feel for holes or other hazards. The house stunk of rot and standing water. Flies and mosquitoes buzzed in the air.

He reached the east side of the house and moonlight came in through the hole in the wall. This had been the sitting room, and an old wooden hutch sat next to the far wall. Glazer walked over to it and ran one hand down its warped and rotting wood. It wasn't even good for burning.

In a room toward the front of the house was an old mattress. Glazer bent down and pushed his hands into it. It was damp from the humidity, but felt like it had been spared a complete drenching. He picked up one end of it and dragged it back into the sitting room, positioning it by the hole in the wall.

He went back outside and untied the horse and led it into the cypress grove, where he hobbled it and took down his saddlebag and the Spencer. Glazer looked around for something the horse could eat, and a few feet away he found some bushes with thick leaves and berries. He pulled the bush out of the ground and tossed it in front of the horse. It bent, smelled the bush, and looked away.

Glazer grabbed his rifle and saddlebag and walked back to the house, entering through the hole in the wall. He placed the saddlebag in the shadow of the old hutch and lay down on the mattress, the Spencer across his chest, one hand near the trigger.

The smell of wet rot escaped from the mattress as he settled into it. Glazer twisted around until he was comfortable and closed his eyes.

§

He cuts across the field, the wheat wild and untended, growing in every direction, large swaths of it ravaged by insects and animals. He sees the smoke first, billowing up into the sky dark as blood, and as he leaves the field the remains of the house come into view. Only a few support beams remain, charred and covered in ash, resting on a hot foundation of smoldering coals. He pauses for a moment, looks at the house and then at the barn, which, miraculously, still stands. He runs for the barn, shouting her name as he moves, his breathing coming in quick, hollow bursts.

The doors to the barn stand half-open and he plows through them and stops in his tracks. She hangs from the rafters, her body slowly twisting with the turning of the rope, her charred and naked body infested with green flies. The inside of the barn swelters from the heat and he bends over and vomits three times. The smell overpowers him, the stench of it all, so strong that he can barely draw a breath. He fights to regain control of himself and as he looks at her the world he knows dissolves away. All he can feel is darkness, a darkness so deep and unfathomable that it has no beginning and no end.

He crawls over to her and looks up. Her face is gone, the skin cracked and blistered. Dried fluid from her eyes stains the remains of her cheeks. Her hair is mostly burned away. He reaches up and takes hold of her feet. The skin is slippery and loose, but he holds on. He thinks of their wedding day, the flowers in her hair, her dress handed down from her mother.

He releases her feet and crumbles to the floor of the barn. He stays there, eyes nearly swollen shut from the tears. His ears ring, but he forces himself up off the ground and climbs into the rafters and cuts the rope and gently lowers her to the ground. He climbs down and goes outside and looks at the remains of his farm, of his life. He begins to search for his son, silently hoping that the boy fled, is hiding in the woods, in the fields. But he knows better. He knows that there was no escape from this, that no matter how swift his boy had been, he wasn't swifter than the evil that was pursuing him.

The boy is behind the barn, crumbled next to a pile of split wood. The shotgun lies next to the boy's hands and he picks it up and sees that both rounds were fired. His son was shot three times, twice in the chest and once in the right leg. The wounds are pasty and thick, the flesh burned black from the muzzle flash. They shot him twice from point-blank range. A boy. His boy.

He kneels next to his son and closes his eyes. The grief swirls all around him and he tries to gulp in air. A vice has a hold of his chest and with each breath it grows tighter. He's surrounded by air and he cannot draw any of it in.

1.

A man's voice woke Glazer.

Glazer felt for the stock on the Spencer and his finger slid over the trigger. The man's voice came again, this time closer, toward the front of the house. Glazer slowly rose from the mattress and crept toward the wall, merging his body with the shadows. He looked out through the hole in the wall, trying to find the horizon. The trees blocked his view, but there was a definite tinge of quickening light and the sky was already a pale shade of blue. Dawn was probably no more than an hour away.

"Put him up against the house," the man said. "I need to take a shit."

"You had to wait 'til now?"

"That meat pie is tearing up my gut something fierce."

"Hurry the hell up," the other man said. "I want to get this over with."

There was rustling as the man moved away from the house, toward the trees. Glazer stayed near the hole and watched the man walk into the cypress grove. After a few feet, the man vanished from sight, swallowed by the darkness. Glazer tried to remember where his horse was hobbled in relation to the man. He couldn't recall.

"Please, mister. I ain't seen nothing." This was a different voice. Glazer could tell it was a black man, but the words came out thick and slow, like something was wrong with the man's mouth. Glazer slowly cocked the Spencer and kept his eyes on the trees.

"Shut the hell up," the second man said. "You brought this on yourself."

"But I didn't do nothing!"

There was the thick, meaty sound of slapped flesh and the black man began to weep. "I told you to keep your mouth shut."

The other man came out of the trees, pulling up his pants. Glazer watched him pass. Once the man was clear, Glazer crept out through the hole in the side of the house and moved along the wall, toward the front of the property. He stayed flush against the house and peered around the corner.

Two white men stood a few feet from the front of the house. Lying in front of them was the black man and even in the dim light, Glazer could see that he had been severely beaten. He wore an old white shirt and dirty pants, his feet bare.

"Pull him over to the tree," one of the men said.

The other man reached down and grabbed the black man by the hands and pulled him to his feet. He stumbled forward and Glazer saw that one of his legs was broken, the lower half of the leg hanging at an odd angle.

The man half-carried, half-dragged the black man toward a tree near the road. Glazer looked at the tree and saw a noose hanging from a limb. Two horses stood near the tree, one of them beneath the noose. Glazer pulled away from the house and fell in behind the men.

They reached the tree and the man carrying the black man let him loose and he fell to the ground. The second man steadied the horse that stood beneath the noose and lifted up a sign that had been hanging from the saddle. Glazer went prone on the ground and sighted in the man by the horse. The man stepped away from the horse and Glazer closed his right eye and fired.

The shot struck the man below the heart and he stood there a moment before falling straight down onto his back. The horse bolted and ran into the darkness. The light from the muzzle flash burned Glazer's open eye, so he closed it and used his left eye to bring in the second man. The man fumbled with his revolver, looking around wildly, the black man at his feet, pressing himself low into the weeds.

Glazer fired again, the bullet hitting the man in the head. Dark blood erupted from the wound and the man fell backward. Glazer stayed where he was, waiting for his vision to clear, watching the road. After a few moments, he stood and walked toward the tree.

The one he had shot in the head was splayed out in the weeds, a bullet hole just under his left eye. Glazer turned and walked over to the other man.

He was still alive, a sucking chest wound moving to the desperate rhythm of his breathing. The man's eyes were glassy and hollow. Glazer pushed a finger into the chest wound and felt air running along his finger. He pulled out his finger and looked at the sign, the man's right hand still clutching it. The sign read DIE NIGGERS in crooked, painted letters. The second "E" was backwards. Glazer stood and looked at the black man.

"This one's still alive. You want to finish him?"

"No, sir," the black man said. "I ain't no killer."

"Suit yourself." Glazer raised the rifle and shot the man in the face. He turned and walked over to the black man. "Let me take a look at that leg."

Glazer ran his hands along the leg, feeling through the pants to where the bone had been broken below the knee. The man winced. "Those fellas do this?"

"Yes, sir."

"Feels pretty clean. Can you walk on your own?"

"No, sir."

"What's your name?"

"Joseph. After the father of Jesus." Joseph's face was bruised blue and his right eye was swollen shut. Fresh blood dribbled down from his bottom lip.

"C'mon, grab my hand. I'll get you inside."

Joseph extended his hand and Glazer pulled him to his feet. He put an arm under Joseph's shoulder and the two of them walked over to the side of the house. Joseph let go of Glazer and slowly worked his way through the hole and into the sitting room, using the wall as support.

"I'll be right back," Glazer said as he turned away and walked over to the man he'd shot in the head. He knelt and went through the man's pockets. There was a pocket watch, some coins, and a few rolled bills. Glazer unfurled the bills and held them up, trying to get a look at them in the moonlight. One was legitimate money, but the rest was Confederate. Glazer tossed the Confederate bills into the weeds and pocketed everything else. He stripped the man down to his skivvies and placed the clothing off to one side.

The second man carried nothing but a picture of himself, dressed in Confederate gray. Glazer tore the picture in half and stuffed it into the man's mouth. He pulled off the man's boots and socks and pants and put them in a small pile. The man's shirt was ruined from the blood and gore, so Glazer left it on the corpse. He picked up all of the clothing and carried it back to the house and put it down next to the mattress. Joseph watched Glazer come and go.

Glazer walked back out front, lifted the corpses up onto the remaining horse, and led it back to the cypress grove. He dumped the bodies and took the horse away from them and hobbled it near a large bush. Glazer stayed with it for a few minutes, speaking softly in its ear. Once the horse was calm, he took off the saddlebag and returned to the house.

Joseph lay on the mattress. Glazer dropped the saddlebag and walked over to him and knelt down and looked at the leg.

"Going to have to get a look at your leg," Glazer said. "Need to see the break."

Joseph nodded and Glazer pulled out a knife and made a long slit along the pant leg, taking care not to brush against the skin. He placed the knife off to one side and pulled what was left of the pants away from the wound.

There was a bulge in the skin from where the bone pressed against it, the flesh discolored from the trauma, and Glazer pressed one finger on the bulge and rolled his hand around the entire leg. Joseph winced from the pain but didn't cry out.

"I can set the bone, but it's going to hurt bad. And you're going to have to help."

"I've seen it done," Joseph said.

"I need to find something for the splint." Glazer walked through the house, but there was nothing on the floor but shattered plaster and bits of small slat wood. Out behind the house he found two partially burned boards. Glazer picked them up and whacked them together to make sure they would be able to hold the bone in place. Satisfied, he went back inside.

Joseph was still on the mattress, one arm over his face. Glazer set down the boards and picked up one of the pair of pants and cut it into long strips with his knife. He then took Joseph's busted leg in one hand. Joseph raised his head.

"I'm going to force the bone back into place, and you have to hold it down while I put on the splint. You let go, and it's just going to pop back out." Glazer lifted the broken leg, put strips of cloth under it, then lowered the leg and put the wood on both sides of the break. "You want something to put in your mouth?"

"No, sir." A tear slipped from Joseph's open eye.

Glazer pushed down on the bone and it made a low grinding sound as it slid back into place. Joseph screamed from the pain. Glazer held the bone down.

"Get your hands down here. You have to hold it."

Joseph put his hands on the break and held the bone down. Glazer pushed the boards into place then took one of the strips of cloth and pulled it tight, quickly tying it off. Joseph screamed again, fighting to keep his hands in place. Glazer quickly tied the other strips down.

"All right, that's it."

Joseph collapsed back onto the mattress, his breath coming out in quick, short bursts. Tears streamed down his face and his head rolled from side to side.

Glazer stood up and looked outside. The sun was coming up, its light breaking hard above the trees. He sat down next to the hole in the wall and opened up the other saddlebag. There was a pistol, some hardtack, a pair of socks and some papers. He flipped through the papers. One was the man's discharge orders from the Confederate army and another was a telegram telling him that his father had died of consumption. The rest of it was pages of scrawling handwriting that were going to be the basis of a letter. Glazer lifted the paper closer to his eyes so he could read it. It just went on and on about some woman named Katherine. None of it made much sense. He wadded up the papers and tossed them out into the yard. He placed the other items and the remaining clothing into his own saddlebag.

Joseph was perfectly still, his face stained from the tears.

"We need to clear out of here. Someone might come looking for those two fellows, especially with that other horse running around."

"I gotta sleep for a bit," Joseph said. "I ain't slept in two days."

"Once the sun is up, this house isn't safe."

"Don't care. I ain't going nowhere."

Glazer looked at Joseph for a moment. Outside the sun was completely up. The backside of the cypress trees remained dark, but in another hour or so the entire grove would be lit up. Glazer thought that the horses were far enough in, but there was a chance that someone on the road would be able to see them.

"You got another hour. Then I'm leaving and you're on your own."

There was no answer from Joseph. Glazer turned back to him and saw that he was out cold, beads of sweat running down his forehead. He reached over and picked up his rifle and started to keep watch.

2.

The knock at the door came just as the sun crested the eastern horizon. Lee kissed his wife on the mouth and walked out of the house, loaded panniers hanging from each arm. Kate looked out the door at the two men waiting in the yard and one of them smiled at her. She closed the door.

Lee walked over to his horse and strapped on the panniers. His Henry rifle was already in the leather scabbard strapped to the right side of the horse. He climbed up and rode over to the two men.

"I'm Eli," one of them said. He pointed to the other man, whose face was still covered by a bandanna. "This here is my brother Bobby."

"Let's go," Lee said.

§

It took them over an hour to reach the remains of Glazer's campsite. The rain and wind had erased most of the signs that he'd been there, but a lean-to was still visible between two low bushes.

"He was here a couple of days," Eli said.

Lee sat on his horse, watching the brothers. Bobby looked at the ground closely, knocking aside the leaves and remaining grass to get a closer look. He found some loose soil and pulled out his knife and opened up the ground. There was a pile of horse manure in the hole.

"He buried his horse's shit," Eli said.

"So what?" Lee said.

"Lots of things love shit. Bugs, birds. Attracts attention. If the wind is right, someone out on the road could smell it. Dog might come sniffing around, start raising hell. This fella here doesn't take any chances."

Bobby walked away from the camp, toward a small path that was little more than a scoured-down strip of earth. Bobby knelt and ran one hand along the ground, over the imprint from a horseshoe. Part of the horseshoe was cracked, a slender break on the left side. He then stood and walked over to his horse. He looked at his brother, grunted, and climbed up onto his horse.

"He ever say anything?" Lee said.

"Had part of his lower jaw blown off," Eli said. "Can't say a damn thing."

"Sorry to hear that."

"I'm not. Bastard never knew when to shut the hell up." Eli walked over to his horse and climbed up. He started off after his brother and Lee fell in behind him.

The path crossed the main road and the men followed it. Long, green grass pushed against the sides of the path.

"I don't know how we're going to track this fella," Lee said. "He went through here three days ago and the rain washed away most of his trail."

"Ain't been a man yet that we can't track. Bobby there's a fucking hound dog."

Did you talk with Camp, get a description?"

"Yep."

"And?"

"And what?"

"Other than 'Yankee,' what'd he say?"

"Said that this fella has a big scar running across his forehead, from his right eyebrow up to the hairline on the left side. He didn't need to say much else. A scar like that ain't gonna be hard to find."

"Most of the men around here have scars from the war. That could be anyone."

"We'll find him. Now that Bobby's on the trail, he won't lose it. We've caught men that hightailed it straight into the deepest swamps of Louisiana thinking all that water would protect them. My brother's got a gift."

The three of them continued along the path, the sun hot and bright. Bobby led the way, his eyes alternating between the ground in front of him and the path ahead. Lee looked around at the trees, the fields, breathed it all in. When he had come home from the war, this was the most beautiful place he had ever seen. But no longer. The two brothers, Hansford, the threat of losing everything that meant anything to him had corrupted it. Possibly forever. He wondered how a man could be expected to live his life under the shadow of such darkness.

3.

Joseph opened his eyes. Glazer sat across from him, back against the wall, the Spencer perched on his legs. It was full light outside and the house cooked in the heat. Sweat ran down Glazer's face.

"You didn't leave me."

"Tried to wake you a couple of times then decided to just wait it out."

"Thank you for what you did." Joseph slowly moved up on his rear, his busted leg jutting out in front of him. "Those two would've killed me for sure."

"Why were they going to string you up?" Glazer handed a canteen to Joseph.

"'Cause I'm a free negro, and they can't stand the sight of folks like me running around." Joseph took a long drink.

"Simple as that?"

"Simple as that." Joseph gulped down more of the water and handed the canteen back to Glazer.

"It's time to go." Glazer walked over to Joseph and pulled him to his feet. Joseph stumbled forward as he struggled to gain his balance and Glazer grabbed him by an elbow and led him over to a wall. "Head toward the back of the house. I'll meet you there."

Joseph nodded and started toward the kitchen, both hands on the wall, using it to support his weight, his lame leg dragging across the floor. Glazer grabbed his saddlebag and went out through the hole in the wall and walked into the trees.

The two dead men lay on top of each other, their skin already tightening up, their eyes clouded over. Flies buzzed around the corpses. The stench of dead flesh hung in the air, and Glazer knew that if the wind turned, it'd blow right out onto the road. There wasn't any mistaking the smell of a dead man. They were damn lucky no one had come along.

He left the bodies where they were and rounded up the horses and led them to the back of the house. Joseph waited by the back door, one hand against the house, his face a ball of pain. He breathed heavy, quick, short bursts. Glazer tied his horse to the old plow and led the other horse to Joseph.

"Which way you headed?" Glazer said.

"South. Fifteen, twenty miles."

"On that road out front?"

"Yes, sir."

"I'll ride with you for a while, then."

"I appreciate that, I truly do."

Glazer walked around and helped Joseph toward the horse. The horse lowered its head and Glazer lifted Joseph's good leg into the stirrup and pushed him up onto the horse. "Going to be a bitch riding with that busted leg."

"Better than walking." Joseph nudged the horse forward and Glazer mounted his horse and fell in beside him. They went past the house and took the road south.

Glazer looked at the sun and guessed that it was around eight-thirty in the morning. The sky was a clear blue and the heat rained down on them as they rode. Dust hung thick in the air. After a mile or so, the trees disappeared and both sides of the road were lined with fields, the ground untended. Wild cotton grew here and there in small bunches, surrounded by weeds and grass. An old wagon sat in a field, one side blown to bits by grapeshot. A couple of cows stood a short distance from the wagon, chewing their cud, staring at nothing.

"This used to be beautiful land," Joseph said.

Glazer looked across a field, at a house that had been burned down to nothing. In the middle of the ruins a faded tarp hung from a pole, like someone had tried to make a tent.

If you didn't cause any problems," Joseph said, "sometimes they'd make you part of a drive team. You'd be gone for a week or two, picking up feed and such. It was always so nice to get away. See the world."

"Not much to see anymore."

"No, sir."

They reached a creek. A bridge had once crossed it, but at some point it had been blown apart. Now all that remained were two blackened support beams and part of a railing. The road jogged to the left of the bridge and ran straight down through the creek. On the far bank, the road reappeared. The sides of the creek were barren, all the trees cut down, their stumps burned out of the ground. The water in the creek was a deep, muddy brown.

"You a Yankee?" Joseph said. He slowed his horse and gently led it into the creek. The horse paused halfway across and took a drink.

"From Missouri." Glazer rode past Joseph and emerged on the other side, water running from his horse's belly. A moment later, Joseph nudged his horse forward and joined Glazer on the far bank and the two men continued on.

"What are you doing down in these parts?"

"Visiting some folks from the war."

"You fight for the Union?"

"I did."

"These folks you're visiting, they carpetbaggers?"

"No. They're Confederates."

"They your kin?"

"No."

"Then why you visiting them?"

"They know why."

Joseph shifted in the saddle, trying to take the weight off of his broken leg. His face winced from the pain. "How long were you a soldier?"

"Three years or so."

"You join up on your own?"

"I did."

"I wish I could've fought. Would've signed up in a second."

"Nothing stopped you."

Joseph laughed to himself. "White folks around here, they catch a whiff of you trying to join, they hang you. Home Guard was crawling all over the place, watching the roads, making sure no one tried to get near the Yanks. Didn't matter what that man in Washington said about being free, if it's words against a noose, the noose wins every time. Folks don't willingly give up what they think is theirs."

Glazer looked at Joseph. His face was marked by pits, and wrinkles hung under his eyes. A thick scar ran down the left side of his neck. Dandruff clung to his tight, black curls. "How old are you?"

"I believe I'm 24 years. The missus claimed I was born up in South Carolina, but she might've just been talking." Joseph shifted in his saddle and rubbed the top of his broken leg. "They worked us hard there in the end, day and night. The closer they thought the Yanks were getting, the more they pushed us. But no one minded, 'cause we knew our time was coming. 'Wouldn't be much longer now,' everyone would say. And it was true. I was so happy I can't even describe it."

The road curved to the west and ran through a thick grove of trees. The shade was a relief from the heat and Glazer pulled off his hat, flicked the sweat from it, and put it back on. Joseph closed his eyes and leaned back in his saddle, his head turning from side to side as if he was listening to music.

"You got any family?" Joseph asked, his eyes still closed. "Missus, little one?"

"I got nothing."

"No one? No family at all?"

"No."

"Sorry to hear that."

"Not as sorry as some others."

Joseph looked at the dust and dirt clinging to Glazer's sweat-lined face and clothing. Dried mud stained his saddlebags. The horse was caked in filth, its hair stuck together in clumps.

"How long you been heading south?"

"Long enough."

They left the shade and continued on in silence, the heat swelling all around them. Both sides of the road were lined with dead fields, the ground hard and barren. After a few miles, they came across the remnants of a long-ago battle. Cannon barrels baked in the sun, the metal rusted and pockmarked. Shattered wagons lay in shambles, the wood burned and reduced to small shards.

There was a large blast crater on the eastern side of the road, the earth burned so black that it looked like glass. Human and animal bones, scored pure white, lay in clumps around the crater. Pieces of uniform were half buried in the dirt, the colors old and faded.

Joseph took it all in and shook his head. "It's a terrible thing, all of this."

Glazer looked at him.

"Had to be another way."

"This is the only way we understand," Glazer said. He stared at the road ahead, trying to imagine its end, and he could not. Just more hills and dead fields and burned remains, over and over again, one after the other. It felt like the entire world was a tomb.

They continued on in silence. After a few miles the road started up a small hill and Glazer slowed his horse and turned around to speak to Joseph. He wasn't there.

Glazer turned all the way around and looked back. Joseph's horse stood in the middle of the road. Joseph was crumbled across the horse's neck, his face pressed tight against its mane. The horse stood still, its head low. Glazer rode back to the horse and spoke to it, thanking it for staying so calm.

Joseph's eyes were half-open and his skin was covered in a thin film of sweat. His lips were dry and thin strings of white saliva hung between them. Glazer reached over and shook him by the shoulder, but he didn't stir. Joseph's horse grunted and took a tentative step forward.

Glazer lifted up his canteen, opened it, and poured water onto Joseph's head. Joseph awoke with a start, the water running down his face.

"You passed out," Glazer said.

"I'm burning up, can't hardly see straight."

"You're in shock. How's your leg?"

"Can't feel it."

"Drink some of this." Glazer handed Joseph the canteen and he stared at it, a look of confusion on his face, before he realized what it was and took a drink. He paused, wiped his mouth, and took another drink.

"How long was I out?"

"Probably not more than a few minutes."

"That sun is so hot. Feels like it's hammering on me."

"Have another drink of water, but take it slow."

Joseph sipped some water then handed the canteen back to Glazer.

"I need to get down, rest for a while. I can't keep going."

"How much further is it?"

Joseph slowly lifted his head and looked around, squinting, trying to focus. He wiped his eyes. "Another mile or two. Just over that hill the road splits."

"We need to keep going."

"I told you, I can't make it."

"You either move now or I leave you. It's your choice."

Joseph looked at Glazer. The water on Joseph's face was already drying and his eyes were bloodshot, the pupils large and flat. "All right," he said. "All right."

Glazer reached over and took the reins to Joseph's horse and they started forward.

§

The fork off the main road was little more than a thin trail of beaten earth. It was surrounded on all sides by half-dead trees and weeds and wild bushes. The trail was so narrow that the horses had to go single file, Glazer turned sideways in his saddle so that he could hold the reins to Joseph's horse. The humid air was clogged with the stink of burnt wood, and as they slogged forward it grew hotter and hotter. Mosquitos and gnats swarmed through the air.

They saw the first body about a mile in, where the trail crossed an old, dry creek bed. A black woman hanged from a tree, the tips of her toes raking the ground. Her dress was in tatters and her body was littered with welts and cuts from being whipped. Dried blood streaked her arms and legs. Flies buzzed all around her.

Joseph saw the dead woman and let out a dry yelp. Glazer shushed him and climbed down off his horse. "You stay here," he said. "I'm going on ahead to see what's happened."

"That woman's name is Dorothy. I knowed her my whole life."

"Keep quiet. If you hear shooting, get the hell out of here." Glazer pulled out his Spencer and cut a path through the woods, moving parallel to the trail. The ground was covered in weeds and a sweet, earthen odor surrounded him as he moved.

Two more bodies were hanged along the side of the trail, both black men. The older one was naked, his body riddled with bullet holes. Part of the young man's face was gone, as if an axe had been taken to it. Glazer looked at them for a moment before pressing on, moving from cover to cover.

He followed the trail another twenty or thirty yards until it ended in a clearing. Glazer drew up his rifle and hunched down and watched. Other than the buzzing of some insects, everything was silent. He crept closer to the clearing and stopped when he had a full view. The ground was smooth and packed hard. On the far side of the clearing was a small building, the wood stained from the weather, but otherwise intact. The frames of four other buildings were visible, the wood burned down to nothing but gray ash and a few pieces of charred wood.

Bodies lay scattered all around the clearing, most of them marred with bullet wounds. A few had been burned. They were all former slaves. The stale smell of blood and shit and ash hung in the air. Glazer surveyed the scene. Once he was satisfied there was no one else around, he got up and walked toward the closest group of bodies. One of the men had been gutted, what was left of his innards splayed across the dry ground. After one last look around, he turned and followed the path back to Joseph.

Joseph sat where Glazer had left him. His head was slack, rolling from side to side, his eyes half-closed. Glazer walked over to him and shook him and he slowly opened his eyes.

"They're all dead," Glazer said. Joseph blinked at Glazer. Slobber hung from his bottom lip. "You understand what I'm saying?"

"You need to get me out of here," Joseph said. His words came out slow and thick. Beads of sweat littered his face. "I can't come back here. I can't."

Glazer looked at Joseph then back toward the road. He turned and took the reins to the horses and led them up the trail, toward the clearing. Joseph looked around in a panic. "What are you doing, mister? I can't stay here. I told you. Take me with you."

"I'm not taking you with me. You're staying here."

As they moved toward the camp, Joseph looked at the bodies. He started to weep. "I didn't ask for none of this. Please Lord, please. Get me away from here."

They reached the clearing and Glazer hobbled his horse and took Joseph over to the last remaining building. He secured the horse and turned to Joseph.

"Going to hurt like a bitch when you come down."

"Please," Joseph said. "Please. This is worse than being hung."

Glazer reached up and pulled Joseph down from the horse. Joseph grunted from the pain, his eyes wide with fear. His dry lips opened and closed, but no words came out. Glazer dragged him toward the small building and as they entered its stifling darkness, Joseph passed out.

The inside of the building was small and dark, the floor made of dry, packed earth. In a corner was a section of an old couch. Glazer knocked its cushion to the floor with one foot and lowered Joseph down, so that his head rested on the cushion. Once Joseph was down, Glazer broke the armrest off of the couch and positioned it under the knee of Joseph's broken leg to take the weight off.

Glazer left the building and took the saddle off of the horse Joseph had been riding, tossed it onto the ground, and led the horse into the woods. Once they were out of sight of the camp, he removed the bridle and slapped the horse on the hind quarters. It trotted a few yards then stopped and looked back at Glazer. He threw the bridle into some tall weeds and stared at the horse. After a moment it snorted and vanished into the woods.

4.

Kate pushed the old wheelbarrow down the thin and battered road, taking care to avoid the potholes and puddles that littered the way. A wagon axle was tied across the top of the wheelbarrow with rope and twine and somewhere along the way, it had become unbalanced. Kate fought to keep the wheelbarrow upright. Jeremiah walked behind her, a gunnysack of bolts and horseshoes and hinges hung over one shoulder, his head down, sweat dripping from his face.

They struggled down the road another mile or so until it ended at a worn-down farm. An old house sat back from the road, its paint long gone, the wood battered by rain and wind. There were signs of rot here and there and two of the windows were missing, the openings nothing more than black holes that stared out into the hot afternoon air.

Off to the side of the house, nearer the road, was a barn. It leaned to one side, the crumbling wall braced with large pieces of lumber that had been placed in the ground and angled up. Kate pushed the cart over to the front of the barn and stopped. She motioned for Jeremiah to lower the bag and he dropped it straight off his back.

Kate stood there for a moment, catching her breath. When she was recovered, she walked into the barn. The inside was hot and stunk of manure. Pieces of metal and wood were stacked against the walls, scattered across the floor. Half-finished projects that would never see completion.

She walked through the barn and came out the back. A large man stood next to a sawhorse, hammering two long boards together. He wore a pair of old, faded overalls, the legs tucked into a pair of new boots. The bare skin of his back was slick with sweat and dirt.

"Emory!" Kate yelled.

The hammering stopped and Emory turned and looked at her. His face was dark with dirt, his hair tangled in knots. He lowered the hammer and turned to Kate.

"What the hell are you doing out here?"

"I have your axle and a few other parts up front."

"Where's Lee?" Emory set the hammer down on the sawhorse and slapped his hands together, knocking away some of the dirt.

"He's after the man who murdered Harold Camp's family."

"Harold Camp is an asshole." Emory walked toward Kate. "This mean Lee's the law again?"

"Just for now."

"Why didn't he come out and tell me?"

"He didn't have enough time. He had to leave yesterday morning, first light."

"One of you should've told me."

"It took us all by surprise, Emory."

He looked at Kate, his eyes narrow. "I never cared much for surprises." Emory walked past Kate and she breathed him in: sweat, piss, and something so sweet that it was nearly rotten. She turned and followed him back through the barn toward the front of the property.

Jeremiah stood next to the wheelbarrow. As Emory approached, Jeremiah stepped to one side. "Hello, Uncle Emory," he said.

"You taking care of your momma?" Emory asked.

"Yes, sir."

"Good." Emory stopped in front of the wheelbarrow and reached down and picked up the axle. He flipped it from side to side, his massive hands slowly moving along the metal, his eyes looking for the seam where the axle had been repaired. He looked down at the gunnysack. "What's in there?"

"Some horseshoes and hinges." Jeremiah said. "A handful of bolts."

"I forgot about those. Grab that bag and bring it into the barn." Emory turned, the axle in his hands, and walked back toward the barn. Jeremiah looked at his mother and she nodded and motioned toward the gunnysack. He picked it up and the two of them followed Emory.

Emory placed the axle down in the middle of the barn. He took the gunnysack from Jeremiah and dropped its contents onto the floor. He folded the sack and handed it back to Jeremiah. "You hold on to that," he said.

"I think Lee has a couple other things of yours," Kate said, "but they'll have to wait until he gets back."

"When's that going to be?" Emory stood still and looked at Kate, his hands inside his pockets.

"I don't know. At least a couple of weeks."

"Who decided that Lee was going to be the law again?"

"Oliver Hansford."

"Just like that? He snaps his fingers and Lee jumps?"

"There's more to it than that."

"Like what?"

Kate turned and looked at Jeremiah. "Go back up and get the wheelbarrow turned around," she said. "We'll be leaving soon." Jeremiah looked at Emory for a moment, as if he expected his uncle to object. When he didn't, Jeremiah walked back outside.

"Must be bad, you don't want your boy to hear."

"Hansford bought the note for the land where we have the shop. He told Lee that if he didn't go after the man who murdered Harold Camp's family that he'd kick us out. Without that shop, we have no way of making a living."

"Son of a bitch." Emory pulled his hands from his pockets and cracked his knuckles.

"He won't be gone long."

"You got a gun out at the house?"

"What for?"

"You know what for."

"There's a shotgun in the bedroom."

"That it?"

Kate nodded.

"It's that double-barreled, right? The one Lee inherited from his old man?"

"He keeps it under the bed."

"That's only two shots."

"You worry too much, Emory."

"I know you managed during the war, Kate, but this is different. Back then, people stuck together. Made sure everyone was taken care of. Now they got nothing. You see the folks that come wandering through town, roaming around like a pack of fucking mongrel dogs, stealing whatever they can get their hands on." Emory turned and started walking out the back of the barn. "You stay here a minute. I'll be right back."

Kate watched Emory before turning and looking out the front. Jeremiah knelt next to the wheelbarrow, drawing in the dirt with a stick. He picked up a rock and placed it into whatever he was drawing. He looked down at his work and tilted his head from one side to the other before kneeling back down and resuming his drawing.

She heard the shuffling of feet and turned around. Emory walked toward her, his right hand in front of him, palm up. Sitting in the palm was a something wrapped in a handkerchief. He stopped in front of Kate and held it out to her. "Take it."

Kate picked it up and turned it over in her hand, removing the handkerchief. It was a pistol. She pulled the handkerchief back over the gun. "I can't."

Emory pulled a small paper bag out of a pocket and handed it to her. "Here are the bullets. I got more guns than hands. I ain't gonna miss it."

"Thank you, Emory." Kate tucked the gun and bullets into the fold at the front of her dress. She didn't want Jeremiah to see them.

"This is about half of what I owe Lee." Emory pulled a wad of greasy bills from his pocket and gave them to Kate. "He knows I can't pay all of it right now. I'll get the rest to you as soon as I can."

"Thank you."

"You need something, you let me know. I mean that. Just because Gertrude's two years gone doesn't mean we stopped being family. You hear?"

"I know."

"Good." Emory turned and walked out of the back of the barn. Kate watched him go, dust trailing in his wake. She ran one hand over the rough outline of the pistol and turned and walked out to her son.

§

The two of them walked back toward Whitwell, Jeremiah pushing the wheelbarrow. Kate watched her son and her heart hitched. What if Lee didn't come home? She had thought that the void of Lee's absence had been sealed forever, but here it was again, threatening to ruin them all.

As they reached the edge of town, Kate put a hand on Jeremiah's shoulder and stopped him. "We need to go by the general store," she said.

Jeremiah nodded and pushed the wheelbarrow toward the other side of the street. The general store was set closer to the road, the only building that wasn't flush with the others. An old, empty pickle barrel sat out front, along with a weathered bench and a few dusty bags of flour. Jeremiah brought the wheelbarrow up to the front of the store and stopped, waiting for his mother to head in before following her.

The inside of the store was clean and well lit. A long center display divided the space into halves, and each had four shelves that held a variety of goods. The bottom shelf of each display was empty and covered with a thin drape. A counter ran along the western wall. James Newbill stood behind the counter, writing numbers into his ledger. He looked up at Kate. He shook his head and returned to the ledger.

"I can't extend you any more credit, Mrs. Sinclair," he said.

"I can pay for what I need."

Mr. Newbill looked up. "You have money?"

"Yes." She walked over to the counter. "I only need a few things and I can pay cash for them."

"I hate to say this, but if you have money, I need to take it for payment against what you owe. I can't carry that balance forever."

"That's not fair. How am I supposed to buy food?"

He rose up from his seat and looked at Kate, pulling down his vest as he stood. A gold watch hung from one pocket. "I don't know. The same as everyone else, I suppose."

"We've always paid you what we owed, Mr. Newbill. Every cent."

"I know you have, but things have changed. Most of the items on these shelves comes from upstate, and they're not extending credit to anyone. You want something, you have to pay for it upfront. I'm sorry, but I don't have any other choice."

"How about if I use half to pay against our account and use the other half to buy some things?"

"I can't do that. Until your account is paid in full, any money you give me is going toward your balance."

Kate pulled out the money that Emory had given her and placed it on the counter. "This is all we have."

Newbill took the money and counted it. He licked his thumb and index finger and turned to a page in his ledger and added a figure next to Lee's name under payments received. He placed the money into a small box under the counter. "Did you need anything else?"

Kate looked at him for a moment. "No, I don't think so."

"Good day, Mrs. Sinclair." He returned to his ledger.

Kate turned and walked back toward the door, Jeremiah following her. When they were outside, they walked over to the wheelbarrow and she took the handles and started for home.

"We can't buy any food?"

"No."

"What are we going to eat?"

"We can kill a couple of chickens, scrounge potatoes from the field down the road. There are still vegetables in the garden. We've been through worse." Kate looked down at her son, saw the worry in his eyes. "It's going to be fine. I promise."

5.

The three men rode through the night, using the light from the full moon to find their way. Lee stayed behind Eli and Bobby, content to let them lead the way. They'd spent the day heading south, and every so often Bobby would stop and look at the ground, study a partial print left in the road that Lee hadn't even seen.

Lee pulled off his hat and wiped the sweat from his forehead. The temperature had dropped a little in the two hours since the sun had gone down, but the humidity was still terrible. He put his hat back on and pulled the canteen off the side of his saddle and took a drink. Lee poured some water into his right hand and splashed it on his eyes, washing away the sweat and salt and road dust. The water dribbled down his face and onto his chest. He let the water sit there, cooling him.

Eli and Bobby stopped and Lee pulled up alongside them. Bobby steered his horse off the road, heading up a small incline. Eli turned to Lee. "We'll camp up there tonight."

Eli followed his brother up the hill and Lee sat on the road, watching him. Eli reached the top and disappeared. Lee looked back the way they'd come, the road slowly winding its way north. He never thought he'd ever spend a night away from home again, but here he was, getting ready to sleep on the hard ground next to strangers. He pulled the reins and started up the incline, his horse moving slowly, its hooves kicking up clouds of dirt and dust.

The top of the hill was flat and ringed by trees and bushes and covered with long grass. Lee slid off his horse and led it over to an old pine tree. He hobbled the horse and removed the panniers and pulled the Henry out of its scabbard. In the center of the hill, Bobby was already stacking pieces of old tree limbs. Lee walked over to him and grabbed one. He cracked it over his knee and tossed both pieces into a new pile.

Bobby picked up a small shovel and dug a pit in the ground, using the dirt to create a fire barrier against the grass. When the pit was done, he lined the bottom of it with kindling and small pieces of broken wood. He pulled out a thin piece of paper, slid it between the kindling, and lit it with a match. Lee watched the paper take flame and bent down and helped Bobby shield the small fire from the wind. The flames slid around uncertainly, then Lee adjusted the placement of his hands and the fire took hold.

Eli carried over a battered coffee pot and a skillet and a rusty, blackened piece of metal meshing. He placed the meshing and skillet over the fire pit and poured water from a canteen into the coffee pot and set it next to the pan. It began to percolate.

"I got grits and cured ham," Eli said to Lee. "That suit you?"

"Sure." Lee moved his panniers and rifle further from the fire, then pulled out a tin coffee cup and a small plate and fork. Within a few minutes, the grits and ham were cooking, the grease in the skillet hissing and popping.

Lee sat across from the brothers and watched Eli cook. The sides of the ham were scorched black, and Eli picked up the skillet and slid some ham and grits into a bowl he handed to his brother. After he put some food on a plate for himself, he put the skillet back on the meshing, sliding the handle toward Lee.

Lee removed the remaining piece of ham and some of the grits. He put the empty skillet on the ground next to the fire pit and started to eat. The ham tasted like burnt fat. After a few bites, he put down the plate and poured himself a cup of coffee and took a drink. The coffee was little more than brown-colored water, but it'd have to do. He set aside the tin coffee cup and looked across the fire at Bobby.

The bandanna was gone and Lee had a full view of Bobby's wasted face. He had been shot on the left side, just below the ear, the bullet blowing out through the opposite side. A section of the jaw bone on the right was gone, that part of his face held together with nothing but muscle. A permanent hole ran from the top of his lip up to his right ear. Through the hole, Lee could see what was left of Bobby's tongue.

Bobby mashed his food down with a spoon, using it to scrape the sides of the bowl. He scooped up some of smashed food and put it in his mouth, chewing slowly. Pieces of food slipped out through the hole, and Bobby wiped it away with his hand.

"How'd you two get started as bounty hunters?" Lee asked as he picked up his plate.

"Didn't have nothing else to do," Eli said. "And lots of people have grudges to settle. Especially after a war."

"I imagine they do," Lee said.

"You were a sheriff? Most towns didn't send their law off to fight."

"I didn't have any choice in the matter."

Eli dumped his coffee into the fire. "Not everyone felt the call to do their duty. Sometimes they had to be persuaded."

"The war didn't have anything to do with me." Lee took a bite of his food. He scooped up some of the grits and swallowed them, barely taking the time to chew.

"You live down here, you have a stake in what happens."

"The only people who had a stake were the folks who owned plantations."

"Plenty of them fought."

"Sure, when they thought it was going to be a grand adventure. Some kind of game. But once it turned into an actual war, the kind where men got blown to shit, they turned tail and got out as fast as they could."

"Doesn't change the fact that every man down here had to do his part. Who wants some Yankee bossing him around? That what you want?"

"My life is the same, either way."

"That a fact? Then why you sleeping out here on the ground with us?"

"Because certain people think everything in this world can be bought and sold."

"Hansford sure as shit found your price, didn't he?"

"Either this or lose everything. You'd have done the same."

"You'd lose your family?"

"No."

"Then you weren't going to lose everything, now were you?"

"You know what I meant."

"No, not really. You know why? Bobby and me, this is all we got, just a couple horses and some bags full of old kitchen supplies we scrounged off some old lady. The great thing about doing what we do is that you always have the power. The person that hires you, they sure as shit ain't gonna do anything to cross you. Once you gun down a man or three and drag their sorry carcasses back to town, even a fucking Jew would cough up the money you're due. No one wants to get shot."

"So you two are just going to do this for the rest of your lives?" Lee finished off his supper and put the plate down. He picked up his coffee and drank the rest of it with three large swallows and dumped the last few drops onto the ground.

"There are always going to be folks that need killing. If things dry up around here, we'll head west, out to Texas."

"I don't even know why I'm out here. You two don't need me."

"No, we don't. But this is the way Mr. Hansford wants it, so this is the way it's going to be."

"And Hansford always gets what he wants."

"As long as he's paying, I don't see a problem with it."

"I'm going to sleep," Lee said. He stood and walked over to one of his panniers and took out his blanket and unfurled it away from the heat of the fire. He pulled off his boots and lay down on the blanket, his eyes closed, getting a sense of how the ground flowed, then got up and repositioned his bedding so that the ground rolled down from his head. Satisfied, he lay back down and closed his eyes. He heard Eli say something to Bobby and Bobby grunted back in reply. He thought about the two brothers, always out doing the bidding of others, and he realized that the problem wasn't that every man had his price, the problem was that some men could afford to pay it.

§

Lee opened his eyes. The fire was out and a cool breeze rolled through the trees. Something had woken him, he was sure of it. He stayed as he was, not moving. After a couple of minutes, he slowly moved his head toward the center of the camp, his eyes only partially open.

A black man sat next to the fire pit. He wore nothing but a pair of filthy drawers, his bare feet covered in mud and leaves. Even in the darkness, Lee could see the man's skin drawn tight over his bones. Lee tried to remember where his rifle was. Down by his feet? He wasn't sure.

The man sat still for a long moment, before slowly reaching down and picking up the coffee pot, silently removing the lid. He pulled the trap out of the top of the pot and scooped up the grounds with his fingers and quickly began to eat them.

Once the grounds were gone, he placed the trap back into the pot and replaced the lid. After sitting silently another minute or two, he slid forward until he reached the skillet. He licked two fingers on his right hand then ran them along the inside of the skillet, trying to bring up the remaining grease. After circling the skillet a few times, he raised his fingers and licked them clean.

He looked for anything else around the fire. Seeing nothing, he slowly half-stood and moved forward, his feet silent. Within a few seconds, he was gone.

Lee turned and looked into the darkness, the same direction that the man had gone, then looked back at the saddlebags by the horses. The bags were undisturbed. He lowered his head and went back to sleep.

6.

Joseph woke to darkness. A surge of panic burned through him as he tried to remember where he was. From outside a small fire burned and its light barely penetrated the door to the shed. Joseph tried to move his busted leg, but it refused to obey, the muscles hard and locked.

"Mister!" Joseph called out. His dried lips hurt as he spoke, and his voice was little more than a croak. "Mister, you there?"

From outside came the sound of boots scraping across hard earth and Glazer appeared in the doorway, his dark profile backlit by the fire. "You finally woke up."

"I'm real thirsty. Is there any water?"

"Yeah." Glazer entered the shed and walked over to an old metal bucket and used the ladle inside of it to scoop up some water. He bent and pressed the ladle next to Joseph's lips. "Drink slow."

The water spilled over Joseph's lips and he swallowed and took a couple deep breaths. "More," he said. "It's like I'm a desert inside."

Glazer filled the ladle again and handed it to Joseph. "You're going to have to learn to do this yourself."

Joseph raised the ladle, his hand shaking, and slowly slurped from it. Some of the water spilled out and splashed on his chin and neck. He coughed a couple of times and handed the ladle back to Glazer. "Thank you."

"It's time for me to go," Glazer said as he returned the ladle to the bucket.

Joseph struggled to sit up. "You can't just leave me like this. I can't barely move."

"I found an old trough and rigged it up to the well. The trough's right outside, and all you need to do is pump the well to get the water flowing. Might still be some rust and dirt in the water right after you use the pump, but give it a few minutes and that'll settle out. Take the water from the top." Glazer stood and walked toward the door. "I had to let that horse go. Someone might come looking for it, and the last thing you want is for them to find it with you. I'll take the saddle with me and toss it out in some field after I'm down the road a ways."

"My leg's all busted up." Joseph said, his voice filled with panic.

74

"What am I going to eat?"

"There's a gunnysack over in the corner. It's got plenty of food. I don't need it. Not anymore, anyway. That should last you a week, maybe a little longer if you're careful. The water's the important thing."

Joseph looked at the dark man in the doorway. Tears slid down his face. "I ain't gonna last more than a few days. The people that did this, that killed my people, they're going to come back and find me here. I know it."

"No one's coming back. Anyone interested in that sort of thing is going to turn around the second they see the bodies. They'll figure they missed whatever happened and keep moving along. You just need to wait until someone sees those bodies and gets mad about it. They're the ones that'll help you."

"That could be weeks." Joseph forced himself up, stretching one hand out to Glazer. "Please, mister, I'm begging you."

"You want a gun?"

"I already told you, I ain't no murderer."

"Suit yourself." Glazer stepped through the door and turned and looked back. "I'm putting out the fire, but there's some split wood behind the shed, along with some flint. Shouldn't be hard for you to get another going. I made you a crutch, it's next to you." And with that he was gone.

Joseph sat there, staring at the door, praying that the light from outside wouldn't go out. But after a few seconds the light vanished and everything turned black. He stared out at the darkness and wept.

SATURDAY

1.

Glazer stood on the edge of the road, looking at the old house. It was small, no more than three or four rooms, the roof caved in on the south side. A yellow poplar grew from the inside of the house and out through a hole in the roof, its limbs growing in every direction. Its leaves reflected the sunlight as they fluttered in the breeze.

Glazer frowned and walked across the road, clutching his rifle in one hand.

The inside of the house was empty, save for the trunk of the poplar, which grew up out of the packed dirt floor. Dry, dead leaves and small branches were everywhere and in one corner of the house was a nest of some kind. Glazer went back outside and wandered the property, but there was nothing to see. It was a dead house on a dead piece of land. No one had lived here in years.

He turned away from the house and walked back toward the road. A wagon slowly moved toward him, an old man sitting up front, one hand loosely holding the reins. As he approached Glazer, the old man slowed his horse and brought the wagon to a halt.

"Howdy," the old man said.

"Hello," Glazer said. He motioned toward the decrepit house. "You know anything about the folks that used to live here?"

The old man looked at Glazer and his eyes narrowed. "They're long gone. Left before the war ended."

"Where'd they go?"

"Hell if I know. The wife took her kids and vanished. Heard she had family over in Alabama, but that might've been bullshit. Lots of folks say they're going one place and end up in another."

"Was Walter with them?"

"Walter?" The old man snorted. "He's dead."

Glazer stared at the old man. "How'd he die?"

"Got drunk one night over at the tavern and started bawling about this and that, shit he'd done during the war. Few minutes later he went outside and blew half his damned head off. Died right then and there." The old man shifted in his seat, looked at Glazer's Spencer. "Thank god he did it at night. That's nothing for women and children to witness."

"Where's he buried?"

"Over at the Old Road Cemetery, back toward town. Why you so interested in the Nails?"

"Just looking up folks from the war." Glazer shifted the rifle so that the barrel was aimed square at the ground and started back toward his horse. "Thank you for your help."

"That bastard left behind a wife and four girls," the old man said, his face growing red. "The youngest was but two years when Walter shot himself. How the hell's she supposed to grow up with no daddy? With no one to look after her, protect her. That man's a damned coward."

Glazer looked at the old man and nodded. "I already knew that."

§

The Old Road Cemetery was about a quarter-mile off the road, next to a large grove of trees. Glazer rode up to the main gate and sat there, looking at the cemetery. It was small and quiet, roughly sixty graves packed tightly together. Most of the headstones were thin slabs of granite with faded names and epithets etched on them between images of skulls and angels. The grass in the cemetery was tightly groomed, cut down short. If there was a weed anywhere, Glazer couldn't see it.

He turned and guided his horse to the east, down a small trail, following the fence. When the fence ended, the trail continued on another few feet before it went up the side of a small hill. Glazer nudged his horse and followed the trail.

At the top of the hill was another cemetery, this one sparse and overgrown with weeds. Glazer got off his horse, tied it to a small iron rod that extended up out of the ground, and walked toward the graves. There were only nine of them and Glazer quickly scanned the faces of the headstones. Four of the headstones marked infants, all of them dying the same day they were born.

He found Walter Nail's grave marker at the back. It was nothing more than a curved piece of wood with his name engraved in it, along with the dates of his life. He was twenty-eight when he died. Glazer looked down at the marker. The wind came up and the weeds in the small cemetery rustled for a moment. The wind died down and everything was still.

Glazer stood there for a long time, just staring down at that little piece of wood that didn't give any account at all of the life that Walter Nail had led or what he'd left behind. He pulled out the piece of paper and looked at Walter's name. He wanted to cross it off but knew he couldn't. For every name on the list there had to be an accounting. Blood for blood. That was the only way to wipe the slate clean.

He put the list back in his pocket and walked back to his horse and rode back to the road. Alabama or not, he'd find them.

2.

Lee Sinclair stood on the edge of the swamp. The water was still and heavy and mosquitoes swarmed through the air. Two sets of tracks went out into the dark water but only one returned. There was no reason to wade out there and dig around. It was clear what had happened.

After taking one last look at the swamp, Lee turned and started back toward the farm, walking up over the levee and back across the field. As near as they could tell, only one person had lived on the property, a widower named Harlan Prescott. There was no sign of a struggle or gunshots, so Prescott either knew the person who had done this or had been surprised. Lee guessed that it was the latter.

He reached the edge of the farm and Bobby stood there, waiting for him, his face covered by the bandanna. Bobby grunted and gestured toward the house. Lee followed him.

Eli stood out front, near the horses. "Anything?" Eli said.

"Looks like he took Prescott out into the swamp and killed him," Lee said.

"This is a waste of time," Eli said. "We need to keep moving."

"Someone needs to be told what happened here."

"Why? If Prescott's dead, he's dead. Finding someone to give a shit ain't gonna do anything but slow us down."

"It's the right thing to do."

"We ain't out here to do the right thing." Eli climbed up onto his horse and started for the road. Lee and Bobby both mounted their horses and followed, Bobby hanging to the rear.

§

Five hours later, they reached the Georgia border.

The road split as they crossed and in the middle was a small patch of land and a wooden building. Lee slowed and looked into the building through a cracked, dirt-smeared window. The inside was heavily shadowed. An old bed sat in one corner and rusted cans and broken glass jars lay scattered around on the floor.

Mounted on a tree to the north of the shed, about twenty feet in the air, was a viewing stand. Lee knew that the Home Guard would put soldiers up into those stands, have them watch the road, see who was coming and going. As far as he knew, it hadn't made a bit of difference. He nudged his horse and continued on.

All manner of detritus littered the sides of the road. Broken axles, part of a cannon, a busted crib, half of a wagon, and rotten, moldy drapery. Lee looked down into the ditch, at the things that had been left behind, dumped when they either broke down or when the burden of carrying them was too much to bear.

Lee caught up with Bobby and Eli, who were stopped along the side of the road. Bobby gestured to Eli. Eli nodded. Bobby dismounted his horse and climbed up the hill that faced the road.

"Where's he going?" Lee asked.

"To check something out," Eli said without looking at Lee. "This man we're chasing probably stopped here for a while, hid out and watched the border."

"How do you know that?"

Eli pointed to the ground. Very faint horseshoe imprints were visible in the grass. They led up the hill.

The two of them sat there and Lee opened his canteen and took a drink. Bobby walked back down the hill and gestured to the road. He held up four fingers and got back onto his horse.

"What's that mean?" Lee said.

"That the man we're tracking stayed up there for a bit. Probably four hours, give or take." Eli nudged his horse and continued south, Bobby falling in behind him. Lee looked up the hill and followed the brothers.

The road was hot and dusty and Lee pulled his hat low to shield his eyes from the bright sun. He lost track of how long they rode, the miles going past in a slow-moving blur of dead fields and blown-out houses. He didn't understand why Hansford had it in for him, why he was always there like a dagger in Lee's back, pressing the blade just hard enough to get what he wanted. He knew that when he returned home there was going to have to be a reckoning of some sort, that there was no way he'd be able to keep the shop going with Hansford as his landlord.

From up ahead came the rattling of chains and the braying of a donkey. Eli and Bobby sat on the side of the road, watching a caravan of sorts pass by. Two armed men on horses went by first, followed by a wagon pulled by the donkey. Five carts lagged behind pushed by women and children, their faces and clothing covered with dirt and sweat.

Eli dropped off his horse, handed the reins to his brother, and walked over to the nearest cart. The woman pushing the cart kept moving, hoping her momentum would keep Eli at bay. She was older, her sweaty gray hair clinging to the sides of her face. A bonnet hung off the back of her head. It was stained a blotchy white with dried sweat. The old woman panted from the effort, fighting to keep the cart moving. Eli walked alongside her as she pushed. He smiled at Bobby and started digging through the woman's cart, pulling out clothes, a small wooden chest, some shoes. The road behind the old woman became littered with her belongings and she started sobbing.

Lee rode up and stopped next to Bobby. Bobby was laughing, the sound coming out of his broken mouth wet and raw. Lee looked down at Eli. The woman pushing the cart finally gave up the fight and let the cart drop. She ran over to Eli and started hitting him. "Leave my things be, damn you!"

Eli laughed and pushed the woman down. She landed hard on the road, tears rolling down her face. Her dress was so stained that it was impossible to tell its true color.

A shot ripped through the air and Lee turned and saw the two men that had been at the front of the caravan riding back, both holding their firearms. "What the hell are you doing!" one of them yelled.

Eli stopped his rummaging and faced the two men. Both were middle-aged, their faces tanned and wrinkled. One held a Colt and the other a Remington. "I asked you a question," the man with the Colt said.

"Just seeing what wares this woman has for sale."

"You know there ain't nothing here for sale. Get the hell away from her." The man lowered the Colt so that it was aimed square at Eli.

"Where y'all headed?" Eli asked.

"I don't have any qualms about shooting you, mister."

The woman was back at her cart, stuffing her belongings into it, stacking them, cramming them into every available inch. She started to push the cart, trying to catch up with the rest of the caravan, which continued north under the cover of the two men. Eli turned and smiled at the woman and ran one hand along the side of her cart as it passed.

"These folks hire you to get them north?" Eli asked.

"You're a mouthy bastard, ain't you?"

Lee turned his horse around and faced the two men. "Let's just put away the weapons. We're pursuing a fugitive that went this way."

"That a fact," the man with the Colt said. "If he's the law, I hate to see what the other side looks like."

Lee opened his mouth to reply, but before he could, a shot echoed across the road and the man with the Colt flew backwards off his horse, blood spreading like fire across his chest. As he fell, the man fired his gun out of reflex and the bullet sailed off into the woods and smacked against the side of a tree. Another shot sounded and the man with the Remington slumped off his horse, his face a bloody mess. Both of the horses that had held the men turned and ran, the reins slapping against their flanks.

The caravan lurched to a halt and a murmur ran through the women. Lee looked at Bobby, who held a pistol in each hand, the barrels smoking. Bobby's horse turned in a semicircle.

"What the hell is wrong with you!" Lee yelled. He dropped off his horse and ran over to Eli and pulled him away from the cart. Eli swung at Lee, but Lee blocked it and punched Eli in the face. Eli took a step back and came at Lee again. Lee punched him in the face and then the stomach. Eli fell to the ground, blood running from his nose.

Bobby rode up behind Lee, his horse at a half-gallop. The horse struck Lee in the back and he fell down onto his hands and knees and before he could get up, Bobby rammed him with the horse a second time. Lee lay sprawled out on the road and a second later Eli was on him, punching him in the face. Lee covered his face with one hand and with the other he reached down and grabbed his Colt. He swung it up and pointed it at Eli.

"One more and I pull the trigger," Lee said. His face was a maze of pain and blood ran out of his nose and mouth. "I swear to God I'll kill you right here and now."

Eli smiled and gestured with his head toward Bobby. "You're not in any position to be giving orders, mister."

Lee looked up. Bobby was a few feet away, still on his horse, both pistols aimed at him.

"Now you listen," Eli said, "and listen good. The only reason you're still kicking right now is because Hansford says we're supposed to keep you this way until he says otherwise. But if you so much as twitch, Bobby there is going to put a bullet in your brain."

"Maybe, but I'll take you with me." Lee tightened his grip on the pistol. He wiped the blood away from his mouth with his other hand. Dust from the road hung in the air and he breathed it in.

"I don't doubt it," Eli said. "Hansford told us all about you, said you're a hell of a gunfighter, faster than shit running through a goose. But I want you to think about something, and think about it good. Once you're dead, Bobby is going to turn his horse around and head back north and pay a little visit to that pretty little wife of yours. And when he's done with his visit, all of that prettiness will be gone. You understand?"

"Mention her again and I'll kill the both of you."

"You're not killing anybody." Eli climbed to his feet. "Now put that gun away. I won't tell you a second time."

Lee watched Eli and knew that he couldn't shoot the both of them. He lowered the Colt. As he did, Eli kicked him three times in the side. Lee dropped his gun and rolled over in pain. Eli bent down and flipped Lee over and looked at him square in the face. "This was your only warning. You understand?"

Eli let go of Lee and walked over to Bobby's horse and took the reins from him. "Go ahead, Bobby. Take your pick."

Bobby dropped off his horse and walked into the heart of the caravan. The women had circled themselves together, the children huddled up next to them, hiding between legs and skirts. Bobby paced in front of them for a moment before he took a woman by the arm and dragged her kicking and screaming toward the woods. Another woman grabbed at Bobby, tried to stop him, but he punched her in the face and she fell to the ground. Bobby and the woman disappeared into the trees.

Lee watched all of this and struggled to get up, one hand reaching out for his Colt.

"You're kind of stubborn, ain't you," Eli said. He took out his pistol and aimed it at Lee. "I told you there wasn't going to be a second warning."

"You're animals," Lee said. He spit out a mouthful of blood. "Both of you."

"You've seen my brother's face. Respectable women, they won't go near him. Hell, most whores won't even screw him unless he keeps that bandanna on his face. So he needs to cut loose sometimes. Find himself a woman and have his way with her without worrying about that kind of thing. Helps him feel like a man ought to." A broad smile stretched across Eli's face. "Go on and pick up that Colt and put it back in the holster."

Lee did as he was told and sat up. He pinched the blood from his nose and spit three times. Once his nose and throat were clear he got to his feet. From the woods came the sharp cries of the woman. He looked in that direction and returned to his horse, which stood at the side of the road, digging at the dirt. He pulled down his canteen and washed the blood from his hands. He poured water onto a handkerchief and used it to wipe his face.

There was another scream from the woods, followed by the sound of wet, sloppy laughter. Things were worse than he had even dared to imagine.

The fact that Hansford felt he controlled Lee's fate cast things in a completely different light, and it was now clear why Hansford had insisted that he go on this manhunt. He wanted Lee dead, had always wanted him dead. It's why he paid the bounty that forced Lee into the army, why he blackmailed Lee into riding with these two madmen. The only question was what Hansford wanted and Lee feared that he knew the answer, that he had always known the answer.

Hansford wanted Kate.

3.

Kate brought the large pot of near-boiling water outside and placed it on the ground next to the rear steps. She sat down and picked up a headless chicken off the ground and dipped it into the hot water neck-first, lowering the chicken up to its feet. She held it there, slowly moving it around, forcing the hot water to soak through the feathers, down to the skin. She hated killing any of the chickens, but this hen was no longer producing eggs. Sentiment didn't put food on the table.

After letting the chicken soak, Kate pulled it out of the pot and took hold of some feathers on its back, tugging at them to see how loose they were. Not satisfied, she lowered the chicken back into the water.

Jeremiah came out of the shed, pushing a wheelbarrow loaded with cut wood. He pushed the wheelbarrow to the back door of the house and started to stack the wood just off to the side of his mother.

"How much more is there?" Kate asked.

"This is all of it."

"That's not enough. We'll have to go over to the shop later and see what else we can dig up."

"Poppa doesn't like it when we take from there."

"I know what he does and doesn't like. Understand?"

"Yes, ma'am." Jeremiah continued to unload the wood. He moved the wood two pieces at a time, one in each hand. "You said he wouldn't leave us again."

"He's not going off to war, he's just chasing one man. And once he finds him, he'll come home." Kate pulled the chicken out of the hot water, shook it, and started pulling large handfuls of feathers off its back. She dropped the feathers to the ground, but some of them stuck to her hand.

Kate looked up at her son. He stood in front of the woodpile, not moving, tears running down his face. The front of his shirt was covered with wood chips and dirt and bits of sap. He raised a hand and wiped his nose and eyes, leaving behind a trail of wood dirt.

"Thomas Lester's poppa promised that he'd come home," Jeremiah said, still staring at the woodpile. He opened and closed his eyes, trying to blink away the tears. "But he didn't. Thomas said he was killed fighting in

Gettysburg, that they didn't even find his poppa's body. They had nothing to bury."

Kate dropped the chicken into the pot of water and stood and walked over to her son. She placed a hand on his shoulder. "Look at me."

Jeremiah turned and looked at her. A few feathers from Kate's hand broke free and drifted up and around Jeremiah's face. "Nothing is going to happen to him. You hear? Nothing."

Jeremiah said nothing.

"He came back to us once, he'll come back again. Understand?"

"Yes, ma'am."

"Good. Head inside and wipe your face."

Jeremiah walked toward the back door and as he went past her, Kate reached out with her clean hand and pulled the feathers from his back. Once he was inside, she returned to the pot and pulled out the chicken and continued plucking it.

Jeremiah came back out and walked to the wheelbarrow. He turned it around and pushed it over to his mother.

"Can I go check the shop for wood? Still plenty of light left."

"Do you have the keys?"

"In my pocket."

"Just be sure you're back before it's dark."

"Yes, ma'am." Jeremiah pushed the wheelbarrow toward the road, weaving it through clumps of weeds as he walked.

§

Jeremiah unlocked the padlock, pulled the chain free, and opened the doors to the shop. He pushed the wheelbarrow inside.

The inside of the shop was dark and the air smelled stale. Even without the forge going, it was blistering hot and beads of sweat formed on his face. Jeremiah closed the doors behind him and walked over to where his father's tools hung on small metal hooks. The tools were old and worn, but each had its place, and Jeremiah knew that his father could grab the one he wanted without even looking. He stood there, looking at the wall. He breathed in the air and captured a hint of his father's smell, the sweet scent of burnt metal that seemed to follow him everywhere. It was still here. But he knew that in time it would fade.

The first time he'd been in the shop was two weeks after Lee returned home from war. Guthrie had brought them out here, unsure of whether or not he wanted to rent the place to Lee. No one had been inside of the shop since before the war, back when it had belonged to Guthrie's boy, Matthew. Although neither man said anything, Jeremiah knew that Matthew was dead, killed somewhere in South Carolina.

The three of them walked around the outside of the shop three or four times, Jeremiah hanging back, as Guthrie pointed out the flaws in the building, the holes in the roof, the rot in one of the walls, the place where a family of opossum had built a nest, and at the weeds growing uncontrollably around the back of the shop. Lee listened patiently as Guthrie listed off the reasons why no man would ever want to work in there, why he should just come out here some morning and burn the place to the ground. Then Lee asked if he could see the inside.

Guthrie opened the door but didn't go in, said it was too hot in there. It was bad for his lungs. Lee walked around the interior of the shop, examining the tools, the forge, the chimney. Jeremiah remembered wondering why Guthrie didn't come inside, why he just stood in the doorway, facing the road.

When Lee came back outside, Guthrie asked him why he wasn't going back to being the sheriff. It sure as hell had to pay more than blacksmithing. Lee smiled and told Guthrie the same thing that he told everyone else — the war was over and he was done fighting.

Jeremiah wiped his eyes and blew his nose out onto the ground and turned and walked to the rear of the shop. Next to the forge was a large stack of carefully chopped wood. On top of the wood were his father's battered leather gloves. Jeremiah put them on. He flexed his fingers, feeling how much space there was between the tips of his fingers and the end of the gloves.

He walked back to the front of the shop for the wheelbarrow and pushed it over to the woodpile. He loaded the wood slowly, taking his time so that the gloves wouldn't slip off. A smile stretched across his face. He pretended that his father was out in front of the shop, wiping the sweat off his face, taking a long drink from the big canteen he kept near the forge.

Once the wheelbarrow was full, Jeremiah pushed it back to the front of the shop. He paused for a moment and looked down at his hands, at the gloves. The leather was black and scorched and there was a hole near the top of the palm in the left glove. He thought for a moment about keeping them on but thought it'd be better if he put them back where he had found them.

After returning the gloves, he closed and locked the doors to the shop and started pushing the wheelbarrow of wood home.

§

The garden covered a large section of land behind the house and was divided between tomatoes, green beans, and onions. Kate had wanted to plant some corn instead of the beans, but Lee convinced her that they'd be able to buy all the corn they needed. She knew that she shouldn't have listened to him, that she should have told him that corn was hard to come by because of all the things you could do with it, that people didn't sell what they couldn't replace. But she wanted to believe that things were back to normal, that it would soon be like it was before the war when they could walk into town and buy whatever caught their fancy.

Kate sat in a row of tomatoes, a pile of weeds next to her knees. Sweat dribbled down her face and her mouth felt like it was lined with dirt. Her hands were dry and rough and covered with small cuts, the nails filthy. She wiped sweat from her face and looked at the tomato plants stretched out in front of her. There were fifteen more plants to go. A week ago, she had put down some white vinegar hoping that it'd kill the spurge and carpetweed spreading across the garden, but nothing had happened. At least it hadn't killed the tomato plants.

She pulled out a clump of carpetweed and covered the hole it left behind with some loose dirt, making sure that she packed it down tight so the wood slats that held the tomatoes were still secure in the ground.

Kate finished weeding the tomatoes and stood up, her back cracking. When Jeremiah got back from the shop, she'd have him walk back through the rows and collect the dead weeds, toss them to the chickens. If they ate them, it'd save them a day or two worth of feed. They had to stretch things as much as they could.

After unbuttoning the top two buttons of her dress, Kate stuck a hand down the front of her dress and wiped away the sweat that had settled between her breasts. From her right came a soft cough. Kate turned, hand still down her dress, and was startled to see Hansford standing on the far side of the garden. His carriage sat out on the road, and he was dressed in a slick suit, his hair combed back, a smile on his face. He held a large white box in one hand.

"Hello, Kate," he said.

Kate quickly pulled her hand out of her dress and buttoned it up. Anger rushed through her face. "How long have you been standing there?"

"Only a few moments." Hansford's smile widened. "I wanted to see you."

Kate pushed down the sides of her dress, making sure she was covered. "You shouldn't be here. It's not decent."

"I have something for you." Hansford stepped closer to her and extended the box.

"What's that?"

"A gift."

"I can't accept that."

Hansford opened the box. Inside was a lace dress, cream colored with small pearls laid-in around the collar. "When I saw it, I had to get it for you."

"You need to leave."

"I was hoping you would join me for dinner. Jeremiah is welcome too, of course. We're having duck. I saw it before I left, and it truly is an exquisite bird." He took a step closer to Kate, the box still out in front of him. "I thought you might wear this."

"Lee's barely gone a day and you're coming out here?"

"Do you remember what I told you during the war, when Lee was gone all those long, lonely years? Your destiny is not to live on this farm, it is to live by my side, surrounded by the comforts that you deserve. I was serious then and I am serious now."

"I should've told Lee about you."

Hansford closed the box lid and placed it under one arm. The smile vanished. "Why didn't you?"

"Because he would've killed you."

"Perhaps," Hansford said. "But I suspect you remain silent because you remain undecided, torn between your heart and your head. Look at yourself, out here rutting around in the dirt like a common nigger, covered in dirt and sweat. What reason is there for you to stay? Love? Will love give your son the future he deserves, the opportunities that only someone of my stature can extend to him? He's a smart boy, your Jeremiah. Everyone can see that. It'd be a shame if that all went to waste."

"I'll never leave Lee for you. I told you that before you ran off to Texas and I'm telling you it again now."

"Things will only get worse for you, Kate. You have my word in that regard. There will be no rest for you or Lee. If you truly love him, you will leave him now and spare him the indignity that is coming."

"Get off my property," Kate said. "I will not tell you again."

"I heard about your troubles down at the general store," Hansford said. "About the debt you owe, how you can't buy any food. I was planning on retiring that debt for you and advancing a substantial portion of Lee's salary. But now I see that line of thinking was premature."

Kate stared at Hansford, not moving, not saying a word. He looked at her, his face turning red. He ran a hand over his mustache and turned around and walked toward the road. "Premature, indeed," he said.

Hansford reached the road and climbed into the carriage. Kate's chest was tight with anger. When Lee returned from the war, she had hoped that this would all end, that Hansford would finally realize she was never leaving her husband, no matter what was dangled in front of her. But it was now clear that Hansford would never relent, would never stop his pursuit, regardless of how forcefully she rejected his advances.

After staring at the empty road, she walked over to the onions and started weeding them.

4.

Glazer stared at an old metal float that sat along the side of the road. The hitch was gone and the sides of the float were covered in rust and dirt. One side was pockmarked from where someone had used it for target practice. He raised his eyes so that he looked beyond the float, toward the trees on the far side of the field. In the growing darkness, the trees were losing their form, fading away into a dark, thick whole that went on as far as he could see.

After looking at the float one final time, Glazer urged his horse across the field. When he reached the trees, he went parallel to them until he found a wide lane. He stopped and tried to see where it led, but there was nothing except a smoky wall of night. He couldn't see more than fifty, sixty feet. He looked back toward the road, but it was gone, invisible in the black. He turned onto the lane.

The lane ended at the ruins of a house, a dead sentinel that marked entry to a large plantation. Nothing remained of the house except for two chimneys, the bricks painted in the colors of smoke and fire. The chimneys rose up from a blackened field of burned wood and melted glass. Pieces of charred metal jutted up from the rubble like black teeth. Glazer guessed that the house had stood at least three stories tall.

The land around the house was scorched down to nothing, the earth dark and slick, like it was covered with a thin sheet of black ice. At the end of the lane was a small carriage, its wood rotten and bleached from the elements, a small piece of the canvas roof hanging from a support pole.

Glazer cut a berth around the house and continued on to the rear of the plantation. About thirty yards behind the house was a partially burned cotton barn and beyond the barn was another blackened patch of land and a large crater. An unknown number of bodies, little more than bones, lay scattered around the rim of the crater. Across from the cotton barn were two slave shacks. Both of the buildings were intact, untouched by the flames that had ravaged the rest of the plantation. Glazer rode over to the closest one, dismounted, and tied his horse to an old metal post.

He pulled his canteen off the back of the saddle and poured some water into his hat and let the horse drink it. When the water was gone, Glazer shook the hat a couple of times and put it back onto his head.

"It's going to be all right," he told the horse as he ran a hand down the back of its neck. The horse was clearly tired. It lowered its head, sniffed the ground a couple of times then was quiet. Glazer stroked the horse's neck, talking to it, telling it that it wasn't going to be much longer now and it'd be able to rest. Both of them would finally be able to rest.

He left the horse and walked into the nearest slave shack. The inside was pitch black. Glazer pulled a match out of his pocket and lit it. Its narrow light revealed a destroyed wood-burning stove, four rotten bed frames, and an empty shelf. Glazer walked further into the shack and searched behind the beds. At the back of one of them was a lantern, its glass cracked on one side. Glazer shook out the match, grabbed the lantern, and went back outside.

The moon cast a pale light over the ruined plantation. Glazer walked away from the shack so that he could get the best light. He shook the lantern, the kerosene inside sloshing from side to side. He opened the top and pinched the wick between two fingers. It crumbled away to nothing. He pulled out the pin that held it in place, cleared out the dusty remains of the wick, set the lantern down, and walked over to the second shack. It was empty, the floor ripped away. There was a hole in the dirt floor where someone had built a fire. Glazer went back outside.

He pulled his saddlebag down from the horse and dug around until he found the shirt he had taken off one of the men who had tried to kill Joseph. He cut the shirt into long strips, shortened two of the strips, and wound them tightly together. He opened the lantern, stuck in one end of the cloth and forced it down into the well until it met the kerosene. He put the pin back into place, shook the lantern a few times, and lit the strip. It flickered weakly then caught and burned properly. It wasn't going to last as long as a proper wick, but it'd have to do.

Glazer picked up the lantern, gave his horse a pat, and walked toward the remains of the main house. Bugs bounced off the glass of the lantern and he carried it low, down near his knee so that the light wouldn't be visible for more than a few feet.

He reached the house and walked out into the middle of its burnt remains. The black and hardened wood crunched under his boots and the stink of burning filled the air. Near one of the chimneys was a large circle where someone had dumped water onto the hot ash, turning it into a black-gray soup that had hardened like plaster. Glazer kicked it a couple times before walking away from the house, heading south.

He found the water pump about ten yards from the house. Its handle had been broken in half, but it was still long enough to draw water. Glazer searched the area for a bucket or other container, but there was nothing. He walked back the way he'd come, this time heading to the remains of the cotton barn. He ducked inside, moving carefully. Even though an entire side of the barn was exposed to the night air, the inside stunk of rot. Old cotton seeds littered the floor and bales of moldy hay sat just inside the door.

Glazer left the barn and walked around its perimeter. He found a dented bucket on the backside of the cotton barn and carried it back to the pump. He worked the pump until the pipe was flushed and the water came out clear. He filled the bucket and carried it back to the horse and placed it near its lowered head. After sniffing the bucket for a moment, the horse began to drink.

"Good girl," Glazer said. He set the lantern down away from the horse to keep the bugs off of it, removed the saddle and blanket, and carried them into the nearest slave shack. He placed them just inside the door and returned to the horse.

He pulled an old brush out of his saddlebag and started to comb the horse as it slowly drank the water. There was an open sore on its right shoulder. The horse sneezed a couple of times but stood still as Glazer ran the brush down its sides.

The horse's belly was a mess of knotted hair, and Glazer did his best to try and brush it out, but it was no use. It'd be easier to cut it off. He set the brush down, repositioned the lantern, and started to rub the horse's flanks and shoulders, his fingers searching for anything out of the ordinary. Finally, he lifted up each of the horse's feet, examining its shoes. One of them was still cracked, but it looked like it hadn't gotten any worse. He hoped it would hold out until all of this was done with.

Glazer untied the horse, led it over to an area where tall wild grass grew, hobbled it, and set it out to graze. He grabbed his saddlebag, the bucket, and the lantern and walked back to the pump.

He filled the bucket with water and started to wash his clothes, using a small piece of soap to scrub them, dunking them in and out of the bucket to rinse off the soapy film and the dirt. He refilled the bucket with clean water three times before he was finished.

Once all the clothes from his saddlebag were clean, he stripped naked and washed the clothes he had been wearing and rinsed himself off. He carried the dripping clothes back to the slave shack and laid them out on the roof to dry.

He stood naked in the moonlight, holster hanging from one hand, his eyes closed, listening to the sounds of the darkness, the night air slowly drying him.

§

He sees the remains of the Cowan farm from where he sits, positioned behind a pile of felled timber. A light, freezing rain falls, covering the burned ruins of the farm and the surrounding cotton and winter wheat with thin skins of ice. Between the smoke and the rain it's hard for him to see more than thirty or forty yards.

Next to him a man named Lewis wheezes and coughs. Lewis is pale, his eyes sunken. He wonders if Lewis has pneumonia or something worse. Lewis coughs into his hand, his lungs struggling to draw in air. When the coughing fit subsides, he flicks away a wad of bloody mucus. Lewis is using a stolen Whitworth and despite his physical ailments, he's been dropping Confederates all morning, sighting them as they pick their way across the farm.

It's been quiet for nearly an hour and he digs through his pouch and counts his rounds. Ammunition is running low, but there's talk of reinforcements and supplies arriving soon, not that it means much. He's heard such talk countless times before. Desperate men always assume that help is coming.

He looks around at the cedar forest that surrounds him, at the other men clumped together behind logs and trees and makeshift breastworks. They're all covered in mud and dirt, their coats slick from the rain. From somewhere to his left comes the sound of a harmonica. He's been in woods like these for an eternity, moving from cover to cover, firing, taking fire, digging down into the earth to escape cannonballs and canisters and grape. Whatever he once was is gone. Erased. How can he ever hope to return to his life after this? There's not even a life to return to. The only thing he feels is a burning desire to inflict harm. Kill man after man, stacking their bodies up to the heavens as if he's constructing some sort of grotesque, bloody tower that will, when it's tall enough, get the attention of the Almighty. He imagines the tower scraping the foot of heaven, the blood and tears and pain flowing upward like a corrosive acid that debases everything it touches.

A cannonball explodes through a cedar to his right, followed a second later by the sound of the cannon that fired it. He looks at Lewis, who hasn't moved, the barrel of his Whitworth trained on a spot on the far side of the farm, a choke point that the Confederates have to traverse if they hope to reach this side of the woods. Another cannonball sails over his head, tears through the trees. Limbs and dead leaves fall to the ground. There's a loud crack as the ball shatters a tree.

A Confederate appears on the far side of the farm and Lewis takes his head off with a single shot. More Confederates push their way into the rubble of the farm, and he joins Lewis in the shooting, firing slowly and methodically, not aiming for the head or the torso but for the gut or the groin or the upper thigh. He doesn't want these men to die. Not right away. He wants them to suffer, to slowly bleed out on the cold earth, their blood soaking down into the deep soil. Staining it so permanently that it will never birth anything ever again.

A cannonball lands right in front of them, careens off of an old tree trunk, and barely misses Lewis. Neither man moves. From behind them come the sounds of a man screaming. They fire and reload and fire again.

More Confederates spill up into the farm, and now they're trying to return fire, wild, un-aimed shots fired under duress, the balls ricocheting harmlessly off the ground and trees. He targets a young soldier and fires, the ball plowing through his gut. The young man takes two more steps before he drops to his knees, his rifle forgotten, his hands clutching his bleeding wound. He thinks the young man is sixteen.

An explosion of grape strikes some of the timber directly in front of him, and one of the grapes hits him in the face, plows a furrow across his forehead, the blood exploding out like a river overrunning a dam. The blood blinds him. He leans his rifle against a log and tears a piece of his shirt off, uses it to staunch the bleeding. He wipes his eyes clear and turns to Lewis and yells at him, asks him if he was hit. Lewis continues to fire, unhearing, surrounded by the smoke from his rifle. A cannonball explodes through the trees and splits Lewis in two. Blood splashes across the icy ground and one of Lewis' hands keeps its grip on the Whitworth as if it still expects to fire the gun.

He curses and wraps the piece of shirt around the wound on his head and picks up his rifle and fires. The trees scream like demented piano wires as they quiver and vibrate from the rounds striking them. The sound creates a horrific symphony. It's loud and darkly beautiful and he hears none of it. His entire world consists of his rifle and the next man that it will shoot.

He sees a Confederate trying to flank and he shifts his position and fires. At the same moment, another volley of grape strikes the ground ten feet in front of him and the balls ricochet up and hit him square in the chest.

It's suddenly hard to breathe and he looks down at where he was hit. His shirt and coat are already soaked through, the blood running down into his crotch. He sits like that for a moment, trying to keep his balance. He falls back, the rifle across his chest. He wonders if he needs to reload and tries to remember where his pouch is. It shouldn't be hard to reach. He needs to reload in case they make it across the ruins of the farm. He will not cede an inch of ground.

Smoke drifts across the battlefield and the air is choked with the sounds of cannons and rifles and men dying. He lies there, gasping for breath, and he knows that this is his end. He feels the darkness waiting beyond the periphery of his vision. He feels it pressing in, closer and closer, and he curses himself. How could this have happened?

He lies there for what seems like hours, forcing himself to breathe. He will not stop breathing. His chest is cold, but his back, where the blood is pooling, is warm. A fierce thirst grips him. If only he could move his tongue a bit, moisten his lips.

A young man appears next to him. He doesn't remember seeing him in camp. The young man is dressed as a steward and wears a green cap. The man kneels down next to him and opens up the bloody shirt and takes in the wounds. He looks at the young man out of the corner of his eyes. He can't turn his head. The man places a hand on his chest and digs through the bloody pockets of his jacket. He watches the man silently. The man pulls out something, a note, and shows it to him, asks if it's from his wife. He blinks twice. It was the last thing she wrote him and somehow the young man understands this. The man in the green cap leans in close and whispers into his ear. He whispers for what seems an eternity and the moment the young man finishes, he looks up and blinks his eyes, once, twice, three times, as many times as he can muster. The young man looks around as bullets and grape crash all around them, but he doesn't flinch, doesn't move an inch. Two Confederates run past and one of them rams his bayonet through a Union soldier who'd taken cover behind a thick tree trunk. The young man just takes it all in and smiles and pats him on the shoulder, then carefully folds the note and places it back where he found it.

The young man stands and looks around the battlefield as if it's some sort of amusement that he can't quite figure out. A cannonball explodes off to one side and showers the area in dirt and chunks of wood and he looks to the sky and smiles and nods, as if in thanks, and then is gone.

As he lies there, he feels the note in his pocket pressing down against him. The weight of it increasing. He knows what it means, what it will unleash. And it fills him with sorrow and rage. Why is this the only way? But he knows it's too late for questions. Far too late. A tear slips from his left eye and blurs his vision. He tries to blink, but even that is too much to ask of his body. He tries to take a breath but it's like his lungs won't listen to him, won't obey the most primitive of commands. The sound of the battle fades away and all is dark.

5.

They rode hard the rest of the day, one of the brothers always staying twenty or thirty feet behind Lee, which was plenty of room in case Lee tried something. He tried to picture how this was all going to end, but he always returned to the same answer. Either the brothers would kill him or he would kill them. It was as simple as that. Lee's chest felt tight, compressed. The only way it would subside was if he got out of this alive, was able to return home. They had the perfect opportunity to kill him back at the caravan but they didn't. But once Hansford sent word, there was no doubt that things would instantly turn.

As the darkness took hold, Bobby led them off the road and across a small field before stopping near a stand of trees. Within a few minutes a fire was going, and Eli was cooking ham and brewing a pot of coffee. Lee sat on the edge of the fire, staring at the flames, not moving. His face ached and his nose was partially blocked by dried blood.

"You want some of this here ham?" Eli said.

"No," Lee said.

"Better eat something."

"I'll eat when I want to eat."

"Fair enough." Eli flipped a piece of ham, pressed it down into the skillet for a few seconds, the fat sizzling. He pulled it off the skillet and placed it in Bobby's bowl. "I can see it gnawing at you, you know. It's plain as day."

"And what would that be?"

"You're trying to figure out what to do with us. Probably planning on killing us on account of what we did back there."

"I just want to get home to my family."

"Of course you do," Eli said. He took the other slice of ham off the skillet and placed it on a small plate. He licked the salt and grease off his fingers and stared at Lee.

"You got something to say?" Lee said.

Eli lifted up the piece of ham and took a bite. "I know you're used to being king shit, the lead dog. I understand that. I look at you sitting there with that scowl on your face and I know that in your head you're thinking about how you're going to kill the both of us without getting killed yourself.

And I'm telling you that you won't ever have that chance. Never. You might as well flush it out of your mind right now so we can put all of this behind us and have a pleasant evening. Understand?"

Lee spit into the fire. "Whatever you say."

Eli looked at his brother and both men laughed. Eli took another bite of his ham. "You're all confused, ain't you," he said. "Part of you still wants to think that what we're doing out here is about justice. It ain't. And it never was."

"So what's it about?"

"Depends on who you ask."

"I'm asking you."

"Most people in this world don't want any trouble," Eli said. He tore the ham into pieces and started to eat them. "But sometimes someone does something he shouldn't have, and that's where we come in. We take care of things, same as you. But the difference between you and us is that you never cross a certain line. You believe in laws. But me and my brother here, we don't give two shits about where the line is, how often it moves, or who moves it. There are no lines. You see what I'm getting at?"

"You're savages. The both of you."

"We never hid what we are. You knew the kind of men we were before we even left town. I know you did. I saw it in your eyes."

Lee poured himself a cup of coffee and took a drink. "And you seem to take a lot of pride in it."

"Just stating the facts. I believe in honesty."

Lee took a sip of the coffee and looked at Eli. The skin on Eli's face was dry and cracked and his hair was knotted and covered in dandruff. The area under his left eye was bruising from where Lee had struck him.

"And this is where we find ourselves," Eli said. He ran his fingers across his plate, licked them, and put the plate down. "We got a former lawman who still believes the world follows the same rules, same orbit he does, and two brothers who like killing and having some fun. But you know what? In a few days, after we kill the bastard we're hunting down, we'll sit down and check the lay of the land. And we'll settle all of this once and for all."

Lee dumped the coffee on the ground. "This tastes like shit, I'm going to bed." He walked over to his bedroll, spread it out, and lay down. He looked at the brothers out of the corner of his eye and saw them staring at him in silence, the fire reflecting in their eyes. He turned over and went to sleep.

6.

A woman's singing woke Glazer.

He sat up. The inside of the shack was dimly lit from the moon and it took him a moment to realize that a black woman sat in the doorway, back against the doorframe, her head turned so that she faced the night. Glazer pulled out his Colt and aimed it at the woman. She stopped singing.

"Do you believe in heaven?" the woman asked.

"What are you doing here?"

"I live here."

"You live here? In this shack?"

"Mostly out there." She gestured to the night and sighed. "They killed my child. Took him from me and dragged him out there and killed him."

"I didn't have anything to do with that."

"I begged them to spare my babe." She turned and looked at Glazer. Even in the dim light from the moon, he saw that her face was dirty and bruised. Her bottom lip swollen. She gestured at Glazer's gun, her eyes still looking him square in the face. "Lord God, he sees it all. Every sin, every wickedness. There's no hiding from it."

"I was only going to stay the night," Glazer said. "Rest my horse, clean myself up."

The woman took in Glazer's nakedness before turning around and looking outside. "The soldiers came and they took him. Ripped him away."

"Which soldiers? Yanks?"

"Our soldiers. That's what the master called them: 'Our boys.' Weren't my boys."

Glazer set aside his pistol and grabbed a pair of pants that had been drying on one of the bed frames and pulled them on. They were still damp and clung to his skin.

"Weren't your boys either, I suspect," she said.

"No." Glazer picked up the pistol and stood.

"That pistol, it bring you what you want? It make you whole again?"

Glazer looked at the gun then back at the woman. It suddenly seemed so absurd to hold a weapon against her. He put the gun down.

The woman stood and gestured to Glazer and walked away from the shack. He followed her out into the night.

"What do you want?" Glazer said.

"What do I want?" She looked up at the night sky. "I want to sit at the knee of the Lord when he passes judgment on the wicked. I want to see their faces when they realize what their deeds have earned them, the look of horror on their faces when they realize what waits for them. How the flames are going to leap up from the pit and snatch them." The woman continued forward and stopped when she was about fifteen feet from the shack. Glazer stopped a few feet away from her. She sat down, facing him. The front of her dress was covered in small splotches of dried blood. "That's what I want."

"I don't think God cares much one way or another."

"This is where they took him. Killed him right here with a hammer. I saw the whole thing. They laughed. Damn them, they laughed."

Glazer took a step forward. The woman leaned back and the moon washed over her and as it did, a pool of dark blood began to take shape across the front of her dress. It soaked through the rotten cloth, saturated every fiber. A dark burn appeared around her neck.

"I told them it wasn't time," she said, "that he wasn't ready to come out and face the world, but they didn't listen. 'The world don't need another half-nigger,' they said." The woman shook her head. "Poor fools, they got confused. Whole world gets turned upside down and they can't make any sense of it, no matter how hard they try. So they did the only thing they could. The only thing they know."

Glazer said nothing. The woman sat in the grass, running her hands over the blades, softly humming to herself. "He told me that he loved me. That's why we were having a son, because he loved me so much. But the soldiers, they didn't see that. Didn't care. And in the end it was all a lie anyhow. He didn't love me, didn't love what was growing inside of me. Only one thing he loved and it wasn't me. He left me here alone and I had nowhere else to go and so I stayed. Before long the soldiers came and said that they'd heard about me in town, what I'd done, how I'd seduced him with my charms, with my wickedness. That I was a witch of some kind. An affront to their Lord and Savior. And by God, they weren't about to let me birth no half-breed bastard. Then they took out their knives ..."

Her voice trailed off and she slowly stood. The front of her dress was now completely covered in blood, from the neck on down. The blood dripped off the tattered ends of her dress, vanished in the darkness of the grass. She placed her hands over her womb and stood still for a moment, hands crossed. She looked at Glazer. "I'm sorry to have woke you. I heard your horse and wanted to come and see who was here."

"I'll be gone in the morning."

From the edge of the field came a sharp rustling. Glazer looked up. The entire field was ringed with dark figures. They slowly moved forward, into the moonlight, and he saw that they were black and dressed in rags. A man was covered in blood. Another was missing his arms. A woman staggered on one leg, the other one gone at the knee, the white bone glinting in the dim light. A little boy stood by himself, staring at Glazer. Half of the boy's head was gone.

"None of us had nothing to call our own," the woman said. Glazer looked at her. "But the one thing we always had was the ability to create life. Even in all the darkness they unleashed on us, there was always that little glint of light and nothing could take that away. Each birth was a chance to create something new, start over. Such a thing is bestowed by the Lord and only he can decide otherwise."

The figures stopped moving. Behind them, stretching out into the darkness, were the forms of untold others, the darkness of their shapes the only thing differentiating them from the night.

The woman swayed in place. The blood was gone. She looked at Glazer. "I don't know how much more of this I can take," she said. Tears slid down her cheeks, glittering in the light of the moon. "I worry about him. Did that hammer kill his soul or just his body? Where is he? The worry is what tears me up inside. I could use some peace. Some warmth. A good place to sleep."

She started to weep and Glazer took a step toward her but a black man stepped forward and placed a hand on the woman's shoulder. Without saying a word, she turned and walked away from Glazer, toward the field. The other figures began to recede into the darkness.

The woman stopped and turned back to Glazer. "Your missus and child, they see everything you do. They know. God help them, they know."

And then she was gone. They were all gone.

Glazer stood there, motionless, staring at the last spot he had seen her. Finally he walked over to the grass where she'd been sitting and he squatted down and placed his hands on the cold earth. There was no sign anyone had been there.

He sat down in the cool, damp grass and wondered how long those specters had been wandering these fields. And how long it'd be until he joined them.

SUNDAY

1.

The three of them sat in front of the ruined house. A noose hung from a tree, and two large, dried blood spatters were visible in the grass.

"Bobby and I'll check around the back," Eli said. "You take a look in the house." Eli gestured to Bobby and the two of them rode toward the back of the property.

Lee sat on his horse and watched the brothers until they were out of sight. He stared at the house, its interior dark, like a shifting fluid. This was the first time the brothers had left him alone and for a brief moment he thought about quietly turning his horse around and riding back north. Get some distance before they realized that he was gone. Would they pursue him? He knew that they would and he knew that there'd be no hiding from them, that they'd track him no matter where he rode. It was better to stay with them, see how things played out, wait for an opening.

He climbed off his horse, tied it to the tree, and patted its neck. The horse looked at Lee with its dark eyes and smelled his face. Lee took a drink from his canteen and started for the house.

It took his eyes a moment to adjust to the darkness. When they did, he saw Bobby standing silently in the back of what had been the living room. Bobby held his pistol in one hand, thumb on the hammer. He watched Lee but didn't move. Lee turned and looked back outside, saw his horse eating the grass. Bobby had a clear view of everything. The inside of the house was still and quiet.

"I thought you were heading out back," Lee said as he walked toward Bobby. He watched Bobby's thumb. It eased off the hammer and a moment later the pistol was back in its holster. Lee continued past Bobby, heading toward the hole that had been blasted in the side of the house.

Bobby grunted and turned to follow Lee.

Lee stopped in the middle of the sitting room. On the floor was an old, water-stained mattress, scraps of clothing, and a couple pieces of broken wooden slats. He squatted down and pressed one hand into the mattress, feeling its dampness. It stunk of sweat and rot. In the corner was an empty saddlebag. Lee went through the hole and back out into the sunshine.

Bobby walked past Lee and stopped at the edge of the cypress grove.

He turned to Lee and gestured with his head. Lee followed him.

The stench enveloped him as soon as he entered the grove. The deep smell of putrid flesh and drying shit. Lee's eyes burned. He pulled a handkerchief out of his pocket and covered his mouth and nose. The smell was like an oil, coating everything that it touched. Lee continued deeper into the trees and found Eli kneeling next to two corpses. Lee gagged.

"This ain't that bad," Eli said. He had a scowl on his face. "Must've seen worse than this during the war."

"I never had much time to pay attention to it then."

"I can't remember where it was," Eli said. "Kentucky or maybe Virginia, these Yankees charged our line. I think there were six of them. Anyways, somehow we ended up back by the cannons, and one fired grape straight into those charging bastards. One minute they were there and the next they were just gone. It was truly amazing. Blood hung in the air like a curtain. Just hung there. I've never seen anything like it, before or since. This is nothing."

Lee looked down at the bodies. Both were bloated from the heat, their exposed skin slick with a foul perspiration that reflected what light seeped through the trees. Beetles crawled over the bodies, and one was covered with small tears and pockmarks from where the birds had been pecking.

"Find anything in the house?" Eli asked.

"Just an empty saddlebag and some scraps of clothing. If I had to guess, a couple men spent the night there. One of them was wounded, probably had a broken bone. There wasn't any blood so it wasn't from a gunshot." Lee slowly breathed through his mouth, forced himself to ignore how the air tasted.

"The one that was wounded was probably the nigger these two were setting to string up. See these bullet wounds? They were dead before they even knew what the hell was happening." Eli pulled a small pouch out of a breast pocket and pinched out some chewing tobacco and placed it in his mouth. He wiped his fingers on the ground, knocking off the loose strands of tobacco. "What doesn't make any sense is why this man would kill two white men to save a nigger. That just puzzles me."

"Camp said he was a Yankee."

"Sometimes I wonder what's happening to this world. I really do. How things got so turned around and twisted up. Niggers running all over the place, acting like they can do whatever the hell they want. White men getting gunned down for trying to restore some balance to the world." Eli moved the chew around the inside of his mouth, smacking his lips. Lee caught glimpses of Eli's brown teeth.

"I don't need to see these two rot down to the bone," Lee said. "I'm getting my horse."

Eli stared down at the bodies. He spit a long string of thick brown saliva onto the ground. There were still so many grievances waiting to be addressed, he thought.

§

They followed the road until the tracks turned off onto a trail, Bobby leading the way, until they reached the black woman hanging from the tree. A crow sat on her head, its shapeless eyes looking at the three of them, the woman's body slowly turning in a circle. The only sound was the creaking of the rope. The crow let out a deep squawk and flew away.

"Why are we going up there?" Lee asked. "We know he's come and gone."

"Because two sets of tracks went in and only one left," Eli said. "That means the nigger is up there somewhere, and I mean to find him. Finish what those boys down the road started." Eli nudged his horse forward, following the trail. Bobby grunted and Lee fell in behind Eli.

They reached the clearing and three crows took flight as the horses approached, abandoning the body that they had been eating. Lee stopped at the edge of the clearing and took in the horror that lay before him. He fought back the urge to gag.

"Looks like someone had themselves some fun," Eli said. He guided his horse between the bodies. "Too bad we missed it. I would've enjoyed this."

"We're losing daylight," Lee said. "If he was here, he's dead."

"He ain't dead," Eli said. "This happened before they got here, by a couple of days at least. No, he's still around here." Eli followed the tracks to the back of the clearing. "Looks like they split up here. Damned nigger took off into the woods."

Bobby dropped off his horse and tied it to a tree. He gestured to Eli with one hand. He pulled out his pistol and vanished into the trees and weeds and bushes.

"Where's he going?" Lee asked.

"To see if anyone's hiding out in the woods. There are some fresh tracks over in that direction." Eli turned his horse and followed the tracks into the woods. "See what you can scrounge up. I'll be back."

Lee dismounted, secured his horse, and walked around the clearing.

Bodies, black and bloated, lay scattered all around him. It was nearly more than he could stomach. He checked the woods for any sign of Bobby, but he couldn't see anything. That didn't mean he wasn't watching, though. Lee knew that the odds were good that one of them was always watching.

He knelt, picked up a shell casing, and smelled it. There was barely any trace of gunpowder. He tossed the casing aside and walked around the perimeter of the clearing. The stench of the dead polluted everything it touched, and he knew that if he stayed here long enough it would seep into his clothes, follow him no matter where he went. And the thought saddened him. Things were supposed to be different now. This was all supposed to be in the past. But he knew that was just a lie, the same lie men had been telling themselves for centuries. Nothing ever changed.

He headed toward a small building, the only one that still stood. Outside the door sat the remains of a small fire, and Lee knew that it was recent. More recent than the massacre. He looked around for the brothers and dragged a boot through the charcoaled remains, spreading them out, mixing them with the soil. He brushed the ground with the side of his boot, covering up what he'd done, and entered the shed.

A black man with a broken leg sat bunched in a corner, trying to hide behind the remains of a small couch. He held a makeshift crutch in one hand, wielding it like a weapon. He was covered in sweat and his wide eyes stared at Lee. The sharp smell of piss filled the shed.

"Are you here to kill me?" The man raised the crutch up, his arm trembling from the effort.

"Keep your voice down," Lee said. "I'm not going to hurt you."

"Thank God," the man said. "Thank God. I prayed for someone to come, and you came. Thank the Lord."

"I can't do anything for you," Lee said. "The men I'm with, they're looking for you. And if they find you, they'll kill you. Understand?"

"Please, mister. You got to get me out of here."

"I'm sorry, there's nothing I can do." Lee moved further into the building, away from the door. "Did you come here with another man?"

"He left me. I passed out and when I came to, I was in this building." The man lowered the crutch.

"What did he say to you?"

"All kinds of things. Please, I can't feel my leg. I think it's turning rotten."

"Did he tell you where he was going?"

"Just that he was heading south, to see some folks from the war." The man tried to pull himself out of the corner, but he couldn't move more than a couple of inches. The pain forced him to close his eyes.

"He shot those two men back at that farm?"

"Yes, sir." The man stopped moving and placed the back of his head against the wall. He panted from the exertion. "Shot them both dead. Asked me if I wanted to kill one of them, but I said no. I ain't no murderer."

"What else did he say?"

"I don't remember. Just that he was looking for people. Please, what does it matter?"

Lee took another look outside. The brothers were still nowhere to be seen. "Listen to me, if you want to live through this you need to stay in that corner and not move, not make a sound until we're long gone."

"Maybe you can talk to those men, get them to change their minds."

"Men like them don't change their minds. You know that." Lee walked over to the man. "Lay back down behind the couch. I'm going to cover you with this cushion. If anyone else comes in here, stay perfectly still and pretend that you're dead."

Tears rolled down the man's cheeks. "I'm begging you. I've lost so much already. Those are my people out there. What am I going to do? I can't walk."

From the woods came the sound of a cracking branches.

"They're coming back," Lee said. "Lie down."

The man slowly lay down, folding the upper part of his body around the remains of the couch. Lee placed the cushion on top of him. He looked around, saw the gunnysack, and opened it. He pulled out two cans and placed the others behind the couch. He tossed the gunnysack across the man's feet. Outside hooves clapped on the hard ground. "I'm going outside," Lee whispered. "Remember what I said."

Lee stepped out of the shed. Eli sat a few yards away, his horse pawing at the ground. "What was all that ruckus in there?" he asked.

"Just digging around. Found a couple cans of beans."

"The nigger riding that other horse is long gone. Probably already back with his people, whooping it up. No way we can get our hands on him now."

Bobby emerged from the woods, looked at Eli, and gestured back toward the main road. He walked over to his horse and got on. Eli prodded his horse forward, slowly trailing his brother.

"This has been a disappointment," Eli said. "Let's go."

Lee placed the cans in his saddlebag, climbed up onto his horse, and followed the brothers. He fought the urge to look back at the small building, terrified that he'd see the man's desperate face staring out at him from the darkness.

2.

Kate and Jeremiah sat in the back of the church. The minister had just finished his sermon, and she wanted to wait for most of the congregation to file out before they got up. A few people smiled at her and mouthed a greeting, but most simply stared ahead, pretended they didn't see her. Her husband had sacrificed so much for this town, but it wasn't enough. It would never be enough. She wanted to stand up and confront them, demand to know what level of pain and anguish their families had endured, demand to know what sacrifices they had made. But she knew better. There was no point to it. They believed what they believed and no amount of reasoning would ever change it.

As the last few stragglers left, Kate motioned to Jeremiah and the two of them rose and made for the exit. The minister stood at the door, shaking hands, and as Kate walked past he nodded to her and thanked her for coming to the service, that it was important to maintain faith in times such as these. Kate smiled and complimented him on the sermon. She thought it was a good message. She led Jeremiah outside.

On the far side of the road, sitting in his old wagon, was Emory. He was dressed in a button-down shirt and brown pants, his hair combed back. When he saw Kate and Jeremiah, he pressed down the brake and dropped off the wagon.

"What are you doing here?" Kate asked.

"Waiting for you two." He smiled and clapped his hands. "Jeremiah, hop in back."

Jeremiah looked at his mother and she nodded. He climbed into the back of the wagon and sat down on a small bench that was nailed to the floor.

"Where are we going?" Kate asked. Emory took her by the hand and led her to the far side of the wagon.

"To a cookout over at Ray and Deborah Mae's place."

"But I'm not bringing anything," Kate said as she climbed up onto the seat. "We can't show up empty-handed, it's rude."

Emory walked around the wagon and climbed up. He kicked off the brake and took the reins. "There's going to be plenty of food. Besides, everyone will be happy to see the two of you. It's been a while." He slapped the horse with the reins and it started forward. "How was the service?"

"It was fine," Kate said.

"I hate that preacher."

"I know you do."

"Everyone else around here is barely scratching out a living and he's parading around like money's no object." Emory half-turned and looked back at Jeremiah. "How are you doing, Jeremiah? Helping out your momma?"

"Yes, sir," Jeremiah said. He smiled at his uncle.

"That a boy." The wagon continued down the road, the sun beating down on them. "Sorry I don't have an umbrella. This heat is a bitch."

"I'm used to working in it," Kate said.

"Got enough to eat out there?"

"We'll be fine."

"You can come stay with me if you want. It wouldn't be no trouble. I got a couple old hogs I could track down and slaughter. Once they're salted, we'd have plenty to eat."

"I appreciate that, Emory. But the garden's coming in and we still have our chickens. Besides, Lee won't be gone long. Only a couple of weeks. We'll survive."

"Might take care of one of those hogs anyways. Damned thing comes after me every time I go near it. I swear it's trying to bite my legs off. It's really turning into a pain in my ass."

"We'd be happy to take some of the meat," Kate said. "But you don't have to butcher it on our account."

"Getting hard to keep animals, anyway. People lose their foundations and they start roaming around, stealing whatever they can get their hands on. I was over at the Derby farm the other day and they lost three calves. Someone came in the middle of the night and just took them."

"I don't think I need to worry about anyone taking my chickens."

"Maybe not. But once the cows and pigs are gone, chickens are next on the list."

Kate laughed.

"That's how things start," Emory said. "I'm being serious. Pretty soon they're busting into your house in broad daylight and helping themselves."

"Like I told you before, you worry too much."

"The last time I was in that church, back when Gertrude was still alive, that preacher gave a sermon about the rich man who came before Jesus and asked how he could get into heaven. Jesus told that man to sell everything and give the money to the poor. The man turned and walked away. His salvation was right there in front of him and he turned his back on it. Now that preacher might be a damned hypocrite, but he was on to something there. If Jesus himself can't convince someone to do the right thing, the rest of us don't have much of a chance." Emory turned the wagon onto a lane. They went over a small hill and continued down into a valley. Both sides of the lane were lined with trees, covering it with shade.

Kate closed her eyes and enjoyed the break from the heat. She knew that Emory was right, that the moment people started worrying about how they were going to put food on the table things would change very quickly. But that wasn't what concerned her. What concerned her was Hansford. The way he had manipulated the situation with Harold Camp's family, how easy it was for him to take control of her family's lives. He had orchestrated everything so that she'd be alone, so that he could continue his advances. In the weeks after Lee went off to war, Hansford had been so insistent, daring even, not caring that anyone saw what he was doing. But when rumors spread that the Union army was hanging plantation owners he fled to Texas. Upon his return he hadn't even looked at Kate, let alone spoke to her. She knew now that he was simply biding his time, waiting for an opportunity to present itself.

Part of her wondered if she should have told Lee what had happened while he was gone. But she was so happy when he came back safe and sound that all she wanted to do was put everything behind her. Pretend none of it had happened.

She looked at Emory. Despite the shade, his shirt was soaked with sweat. Maybe she could tell him about Hansford, what he was doing. She knew that Emory wouldn't judge her, that he would stand beside her no matter what. But she hated the idea of asking anyone else for help. She had made it through the worst of the war and she would make it through this. Once Lee was back in a week or so, they would decide what they were going to do, even if it meant moving away. But she would never again allow her family to be controlled by Hansford. That man had done enough damage.

The wagon pulled away from the trees. Fields lined both sides of the road, the wheat wild and barely tended. A group of black men walked the fields, machetes in hand, trying to trim back the weeds. None of them looked up as the wagon went by.

3.

Glazer looked at the drawing of the woman in the ad. She smiled slightly, a little flourish by the artist. He imagined that her hair was brown, that the dress was a pale yellow. He wished that he could remember what her voice sounded like. The way she said his name. He'd give anything to hear that voice one more time. To hear it sing.

He carefully folded the ad and placed it in his breast pocket. He sat next to a large oak tree, the Spencer in one hand. Shadows from the tree covered him, and firebushes enclosed him on two sides. Someone would have to be standing right next to him before they'd see him. His horse was hobbled a mile away, hidden in an old cotton barn. The fields surrounding the barn hadn't been tilled in years.

He looked at the small house, which was about forty yards away. It was nicely painted, with new windows. A bit further down the road was the main plantation house, the front yard filled with children and women enjoying the afternoon. Between the two homes was a line of willow trees. The lawn around the plantation house was green and cut short.

The man who lived in the small house was named Patrick Doyle. He worked as the field manager for the owner of the plantation. An hour or so earlier, a black man had come to the door and Patrick left with him. Patrick had a wife and two daughters. One of the daughters came outside and started to skip around the yard. She wore a faded blue dress. Glazer guessed that she was six or seven.

Glazer silently moved to the other side of the tree, closer to the bushes, never losing sight of the little girl. His new position gave him a full view of the main house. Behind the house was a large barn and four sheds. Black men and women worked in the cotton fields. There was no sign of Patrick. He saw no white men, only the women out front. He wondered if all the men had been killed in the war or had simply run off. Either seemed likely.

He sat next to the bushes for at least an hour, remaining perfectly still, watching the plantation. He counted five white women and eight kids. It was hard to estimate the number of black, but he guessed it was at least twenty. He glimpsed Patrick a few times, on the edge of the field, yelling and waving his arms at the workers. There was no rest, not even on the Sabbath.

Glazer returned to his original position near the tree. Both girls now played in the front yard, skipping and chasing each other, clasping their hands together and spinning in circles. Their mother stood right outside the front door, a glass of tea in one hand. Glazer studied their faces. There was nothing there but joy and peace. The worst was over for them and they could finally breathe. Life had returned to normal.

Glazer put the Spencer down in some tall grass by the tree. He removed his holster and placed it next to the rifle. After making sure that both weapons were hidden by the grass, he walked out toward the road, angling his approach so that no one would be able to see him come out of the trees.

He walked down the middle of the road, toward the plantation. When he reached the lane that ran perpendicular to the road, he turned onto it. The women out front watched him as he approached. Glazer nodded to them and tipped his hat. One of them waved.

Behind the house, black men and women sat on a worn bench. They were surrounded by wooden crates, each stuffed with thick wads of cotton. They ran their fingers through the cotton, picking out the seeds. Glazer walked toward them. "Who's in charge here?"

One of the men looked at Glazer. He had a small piece of wood in his mouth and he pulled it out and pointed toward the field. "The boss man is out in the cotton somewhere. His name is Mister Patrick. You lookin' for work?"

"Just hoping to earn a meal is all."

"He ain't much one for charity, earned or not. But he can talk to you about that." The man returned the wood to his mouth and returned to his work. "Head on out there. You'll see him."

"I appreciate it," Glazer said. A hot wind blew in from the field, filling the air with dirt and small pieces of cotton. Glazer walked to the edge of the field and looked for Patrick. He finally found him about forty rows down, bent over, tearing at the ground with what looked like a shovel. Glazer followed the edge of the field. Three black women walked past him, but he didn't look at them. He kept his eyes on Patrick.

A black man saw Glazer coming down the row and he tapped Patrick on the shoulder. He stood and looked at Glazer. He was covered in dust and pieces of cotton. The knuckles on his right hand bled.

"You Mister Patrick?" Glazer asked as he approached.

"Who are you?" Patrick brushed the dirt off his pants.

"I'm looking for work."

"I got all the help I need."

"Not looking for any money, just some supper. I'd be happy to work the rest of the day."

"You ever hoed cotton?"

"I've seen it done."

"You sound like a carpetbagger."

"I'm from Missouri."

"That doesn't settle much. Missouri went both ways."

"You hear of the Missouri Guards?"

"Colonel Garland was one of the commanders of that outfit, wasn't he?"

"I never met him personally, but everyone spoke very highly of him." Glazer looked Patrick square in the eye. "He never did us wrong."

"Where'd you fight?"

"Bunch of places, but the biggest battle I saw was for Nashville. Gave those bastards hell but it wasn't enough. After that I joined up with General Johnston and went down to Carolina."

"I don't have any money. Can barely afford the help I got."

"Like I said, I don't want any money. Give me some supper and we'll be square."

"If you hoe the rest of the day, I'll make sure my wife fixes something decent for you. How's that sound?"

"More than fair."

"Abraham here will get you a hoe, assign you some rows. You don't finish, you don't eat. Got it?"

"That won't be a problem."

"Good." Patrick waved Glazer off and Abraham led him toward a storage shed. Within a few minutes, Glazer was at work deep in the cotton.

4.

Eli and Lee rode side by side, with Bobby lagging about ten yards behind them.

On the western horizon dark storm clouds gathered and lightning flared across the underbelly of the clouds. The humidity was unbearable and the back of Lee's shirt was soaked down to the skin. He wished the rain would hurry up and get here, give them some relief.

"We're only a day or so behind him now," Eli said.

"What are we going to do when we find him?" Lee asked.

"Kill him. What else?"

"That's not what I mean. Are we going to try and get him in the middle of the night, ambush him out on the road, or what?"

"Hadn't really thought about it."

"Maybe we should. I don't want to get shot."

"You're trying to complicate something that doesn't need to be complicated. This guy doesn't know us, doesn't even know anyone's after him. We'll take a quick look at things to get our bearings. If things look how I expect them to, we'll walk up and shoot him. Nice and simple."

"Nice and simple."

"That's right. I got no qualms about shooting a man in the back." Eli spit and turned to Lee. "I've done it before and I'll do it again."

Lee returned his gaze to the road. The sky continued to grow dark and the wind picked up. They reached the base of a hill and started up, the horses panting in the heat. Lee rubbed his horse's neck.

They topped the hill and continued on. A light rain began to fall, the drops disintegrating when they hit the hard, dry ground. Up ahead, near two tall elm trees, stood six men. Two horses were tied to the trees. As they neared the men, Lee saw that they were Union soldiers, their blue uniforms worn and faded and covered in road dust. One of the soldiers walked out onto the road and unslung the rifle that had been on his back. He placed the barrel across his left arm, his right hand near the trigger.

"What've we got here?" Eli said.

"Nothing that concerns us," Lee said. "We'll see what they want and keep going."

"Been a while since I killed a Blue Belly."

Lee shook his head, but didn't say anything. What was there to say?

As they closed in on the soldiers, the one on the road whistled and the other soldiers came out and joined him. Sections of their uniforms were hastily patched with brown- and black-colored cloth. They formed a wide semicircle around the soldier with the rifle, blocking the road.

Eli and Lee stopped in front of the soldier with the rifle, Bobby staying behind them. Lee took off his hat and wiped his brow. The soldier with the rifle looked at him before turning his attention to the two brothers.

"You mind getting the hell out of the way?" Eli said.

"Where you fellas headed?" the soldier with the rifle asked. The right side of his face was scarred with ropy, pink tissue from where it had been burned. The light rain continued to fall.

"We're after a fugitive," Eli said. "A murderer."

"You really expect me to believe you three pieces of shit are the law?"

"I'm a sheriff up in Tennessee," Lee said. He pulled his badge out of his pocket and tossed it to the soldier. "These two men were hired to accompany me."

The soldier glanced at the badge. "You boys are a long ways from home."

"So are you," Eli said, he took his hat off, hung it on the horn of his saddle. The rain slowly trickled down his dry, dirty face.

"This badge don't mean shit." The soldier tossed it back to Lee. "I can slip on a general's coat but that doesn't mean I am one."

"We just want to catch the man we're after and return home."

"This man we're hunting, he's a Yankee," Eli said. "Loves butchering women and children. Maybe you boys know him. Maybe he's a friend of yours."

"You bastards never learn, do you," one of the other soldiers said. "Get your asses whipped and you still feel entitled to run your mouths."

"See, shit like that's how you get yourself into trouble," Eli said.

"We have the legal authority to shoot you where you stand," the soldier said. "You should think about that before you open that mouth of yours again."

Lee looked over at the trees, where the horses were tied. Between the two trees sat a small, two-wheeled wagon. An old drape covered most of the wagon, but near the front several silver items jutted out from under the covering. Two candelabras, a large bowl, the hilt of a sword. Lee turned back to the soldiers. The one with the rifle looked at him, the soldier's face cold and expressionless.

"Those are nice horses," a soldier in the back said. "I especially like that gelding." He gestured to Eli's horse. "Looks nice and calm."

The rain picked up in intensity, but it provided no relief. Sweat rolled down Lee's face. The soldiers slowly spread further apart. Lee reached forward and flipped the buckle off the scabbard that held his Henry.

"I got this horse from my old man," Eli said. "He was a mean son of a bitch. He had this willow branch — the damned thing had to be four feet long — and he used to whip my ass something fierce with it. Sometimes I think he whipped me just for the practice. I still have the scars. But he never used it on my brother." Eli smiled at the soldiers, who were all looking at him. "He used the shovel on my brother. Would come up behind him and waylay him in the back of the fucking head and knock him out cold. Sometimes he'd follow that up with one across the back. You see that and you're glad to get the willow branch, welts or no welts. Nobody wants to get a shovel up the side of the head."

Bobby fired his rifle. It was still in the scabbard, angled up so that the barrel faced forward. The shot struck the soldier with the rifle on the right side of his chest. The soldier stood there, his face blank, struggling to raise his weapon. He fired a wild shot that vanished in the rain, teetered back and forth a bit, and fell face-first onto the road.

The remaining soldiers reached for their guns. Lee pulled out his Colt and shot the nearest one in the face. He sighted in another soldier and fired and hit him in the chest. One of the other soldiers returned fire and struck Lee's horse on the left side of the neck. The horse shrieked and dropped down onto its front knees. Its hind legs quivered for a moment, struggling to maintain its weight, then the legs gave out and the horse tilted hard to the right. As it collapsed, Lee jumped out of the saddle, trying to get clear.

The horse landed on its side, dark blood instantly pooling under its neck. The rain fell and the horse stared up at the sky, unsure of what happened. It snorted several times and fell silent. Lee got up and ran back to the dead horse, using it as cover. Several bullets struck its side. The sound was like meat being cleaved.

Eli fired and the bullet struck one of the soldiers on the right side, below the armpit, and the soldier spun around and dropped to his knees. Eli fired two more times, shooting the same soldier in the groin and the left leg.

The two remaining soldiers ran for the trees, trying to get behind cover. Bobby now had his Sharps rifle out and he fired at them as fast as he could reload, the bullets tearing through the ground, kicking up water and mud. The soldiers reached one of the trees and dropped behind it, returning fire. Bobby continued to shoot, blowing chunks of bark off the tree. Smoke rolled across the road.

Lee tried to pull his Henry out from beneath his horse, but it wouldn't budge. He stayed behind the horse, eyes on the trees, watching to see if either of the soldiers was going to leave their cover.

Bobby flanked wide, driving his horse out into the field. Eli dropped off his horse and whacked it on the back. It trotted away and Eli stood in the middle of the road, a pistol in each hand. "You stupid motherfuckers!" he said.

One of the soldiers leaned out from behind the tree and fired on Eli. Eli lowered himself down to a knee and returned fire with both pistols. Several rounds struck the soldier in the chest and face and he crumbled to the ground, the rain smearing his blood across the ground.

Lee stood up and ran across the road, staying low, eyes surveying the land.

Eli walked toward the trees, reloading his pistols as he moved. "It's all over for you," Eli said. "Might as well come on out here, face what's coming like a man."

"Fuck you, you damned Graybacks!" the soldier yelled.

Two quick shots from Bobby's Sharps echoed across the road and the soldier stumbled away from the trees. He opened his mouth and blood spilled out. After taking another step he collapsed. His entire back was soaked red from where he had been shot, his eyes turning glassy and hard, his mouth opening and closing silently. Then he was still.

Lee stood on the road, his Colt up, eyes on Eli's back. If he took Eli now, he might be able to catch Bobby before he knew what was happening.

Before Lee could act, Bobby rode up from behind the trees and came around onto the road, his horse kicking and panting. His eyes were locked onto Lee, the Sharps up and ready. Lee holstered his Colt and Bobby dropped down off his horse and started to search the dead soldiers for anything that might be useful.

Eli holstered his pistols and walked over to the wagon. "Give me a hand with this," he said to Lee. Eli held part of the drape that covered the back of the wagon.

Lee went to the other side of the wagon and grabbed a corner of the drape and the two of them pulled it back. The rain was hard and steady. They dropped the drape into a heap and looked into the back of the wagon.

Two men and a woman lay inside. The woman had been shot in the chest, the dried blood around the wound purple and gelatinous. The men's throats had been slashed, their pockets turned out. Black bugs crawled over them. Both men were missing their boots.

Toward the front of the wagon, near the candelabras and the bowl, sat two large trunks. Clothes lay scattered around the trunks. Eli opened one of them. It was filled with guns and silverware and pieces of jewelry. He picked up some of the jewels and ran his fingers over them.

"Look at this," Eli said.

Lee walked over to Eli and looked into the trunk. It was obvious that the soldiers had been at it for a while, probably hitting travelers and isolated farms. If Lee had to guess, they carried the bodies with them for a while and dumped them far from where the actual crime had taken place. Unless there were bodies sprawled out across the road, no one had any reason to suspect that anything amiss had happened.

"How do you want to divide this up?" Eli asked.

"What do you mean?"

"These jewels are worth a lot of money."

"I'm not taking any of that."

"C'mon, now. You tellin' me that this might not change more than a few things for you back home?"

Lee knew that Eli was right, that those jewels might change some things, but they couldn't change what mattered. They couldn't get him out of this mess with the brothers, they couldn't ensure that when he got home Hansford would leave his family alone. What did Hansford care about some jewels? That man still had more than enough money to buy and sell Whitwell several times over.

"I'm not stealing from these people," Lee said.

"The stealing's already been done, and the folks who owned this stuff are dead. You think it's going to miraculously find its way back to their kin if we leave it here? We both know this wagon will be picked clean, and not a single person doing the picking will have a shred of regret."

"Do whatever you're going to do. I'm going to get my things from my horse." Lee walked back to his dead horse. The rain dropped off and was now just a drizzle.

Bobby knelt next to Lee's horse. One of Bobby's hands was on the animal's neck and Lee saw that its eyes were now closed. Lee stopped next to Bobby. He looked up at Lee and grunted, gesturing back to the horse. Lee nodded. Bobby ran a hand down the horse's neck, his fingers combing the wet mane, his touch soft and gentle. Lee watched Bobby and didn't know what to make of this. How could one be so cruel and yet so gentle?

Bobby bowed his head for a moment. When he opened his eyes, he patted the horse one last time, stood, and walked away.

5.

When the pot reached a hard boil, Kate dropped in cut cabbage and carrots and corn and potatoes. She placed the lid on the pot, let it boil a little longer, then lifted the pot off the stove and carried it outside.

Two tables sat near a roasting pit, just off the drive that came up to the house. Emory and his cousin Ray Derby and Ray's wife Deborah Mae and her sister Eva stood near the tables. Ray tended to a small hog that roasted over the pit. He used a small, worn brush to spread melted fat and butter across the pig's skin. Kate placed the pot on a flat rock that sat in the middle of one of the tables. She lifted the lid, looked inside, then replaced the lid. "It just needs to sit for another five or ten minutes."

Emory watched the kids play and took a sip of sweet tea. "I love seeing that," he said. "Just running around, having fun. Not a care in the world. Makes me wish I was a kid again."

"When you were that age," Ray said, "you were stealing everything that wasn't nailed down."

"Just a few essentials," Emory said, a smile on his face. "Besides it was different back then."

"Different because you were the one doing it?" Ray said. He laughed as he brushed the hog. "You'd go running down the middle of the street like a bat out of hell, then at the last minute cut over and steal whatever fruit was sitting out in front of old man Newbill's store."

"I was hungry!"

"Should've gotten your ass out in that field and helped your old man."

"Nah," Emory said. "He did just fine without me."

"Why do all your stories revolve around stealing?" Deborah Mae said. "You two make it sound like you were desperados or something."

"It was fun and an apple here and there didn't hurt nobody," Emory said. "'Sides, once I was grown I more than paid back what I stole. I think Newbill always added an extra cent to my bill to make up the difference. Cheap bastard."

Eva stared off. Her face flat. Kate touched her hand. "Are you all right?"

She looked at Kate, her eyes narrow. She pulled her hand away and walked toward the house.

"I didn't upset her, did I?" Kate said.

"She's having a rough time," Deborah Mae said. "William's really acting up and with things as tight as they are, well, you know."

"I'm very sorry to hear that."

"A boy needs a man in his life," Ray said. "A father. The threat of a good ass-whipping is about the only thing that will keep a kid like William from running wild."

"Ray," Deborah Mae said.

"It's the truth." He dipped the brush in the can that held the fat and butter and stirred it.

"Donnie was a good man," Kate said.

"Amen to that," Emory said. "He was a fine man."

"Me and him used to go fishing down at the creek," Ray said as he stroked the pig with the brush, "over there by Hollow Bend. Anyway, there was a section of the field we had to cross that sat at the bottom of a hill. This crazy bastard lived in a shack up on that hill, and every time he saw us, he'd open fire with that double-barrel of his. Pellets and shot bouncing all over the damned place. He was far enough away that we weren't in any real danger, but damned if it wasn't annoying as all hell. Both ways, in and out, we'd have to avoid that old man's buckshot.

"Donnie kept talking about how he was going to go up there and bust that old man's legs in the middle of the night, burn his shack down, shit like that." Ray chuckled to himself. "That was just talk. But one day he brought his old musket with him and when that old man fired, Donnie fired right back. He was laughing his ass off, reloading that thing as fast as he could, determined to keep that old man pinned. After a few minutes of this, the old man started yelling, begging us to stop, saying he'd never shoot at us again. I never laughed so hard in my whole damn life. You shoulda seen the look on that old bastard's face when that first ball hit the side of his porch. I bet he about shit himself."

Kate was laughing along with everyone else when something struck her across the face. She put a hand against her cheek and looked up. Eva stood over her, face burning red, her chest rising and falling with each breath.

"Don't you dare laugh," Eva said. "Don't you dare laugh at my husband."

"Eva!" Ray shouted. "What's gotten into you?"

"I - I didn't mean any offense," Kate said. She pulled her hand away and looked at it as if she expected to find blood.

"You sit there all prim and proper," Eva said, her eyes glaring at Kate, "without a care in the world. And you have the nerve to laugh at my husband? You're not even a blood relation." Eva swayed from side to side, as if she was struggling to keep her balance in the face of her rage.

"Eva, that's enough!" Emory said.

She glared at him. "Just because you were married to Lee's sister doesn't mean a damned thing. Why is Kate even here? I didn't ask her to come. And yet here she sits. Eating our food, drinking our water. My husband is dead, Emory. I don't even know where he's buried. You know what that's like? And I'm expected to stand by and tolerate this kind of insult?"

"Perhaps you should leave," Deborah Mae said to Kate.

"Now hold on one second," Emory said. "Kate didn't do anything to deserve this treatment."

"It's all right," Kate said. She got up and headed toward the barn where Jeremiah was playing with the other children. Emory shook his head and followed her.

"Eva's just acting out," he said. "She'll calm down."

"Someone like that doesn't calm down." Kate stopped and looked at him. "She slapped me, Emory. What if Jeremiah had seen that? He has enough on his mind the way it is."

"I'll get the wagon."

"We can walk."

"I brought you here and I'm taking you home. I'll meet you out on the road." He turned and walked toward the far side of the house, where his horse was hitched, his face down, one hand rubbing his forehead.

She watched him for a moment before looking back toward the table. Deborah Mae had her hands on Eva's shoulders, trying to calm her down. Eva thrashed against Deborah Mae, screaming and yelling. Ray stood next to the pig, slowly brushing it, his back to the women.

Kate closed her eyes, her face still burning from the slap. She forced herself to breathe deeply and slowly through her nose. It seemed as if none of this was ever going to end. The fear, the anger. The jealousy over husbands who were lucky enough to come home. The sons cursed to grow up without their fathers. She didn't know how the world was going to continue in the face of all of that.

6.

The sun sat low on the western horizon and Glazer stood and leaned back, trying to loosen the muscles in his back. He looked around the cotton, at the black workers as they slowly walked out of the field. Most of the men wore no shirts, the reddish flesh of their old scars clearly visible. Glazer followed them.

Patrick stood at the supply shed, watching the workers return their tools, marking them off one by one in a small pad he kept. Glazer stood off to one side, waiting until the other men were finished. When the last man walked away, Glazer went up to the shed.

"Where do you want this?" Glazer asked.

"Just put it in against one of the walls," Patrick said.

Glazer entered the shed, placed the hoe against the back wall, and stepped back outside.

"I didn't catch your name," Patrick said.

"It's Samuel," Glazer said. "Samuel Perkins."

"I'm Patrick Doyle. Head over to the house and get washed up. There's a pump around back. I'll be there in a couple minutes." He closed the door to the shed, ran a chain through the door handles, and locked it with a large, rusted lock. "You more than earned some supper."

Glazer took off his shirt and started for the house. The black workers mingled together near their quarters, several of them watching Glazer. None had spoken to him during the day, unsure of what to make of him. The crazy white man who came in off the road with nothing and asked for work, who didn't want any money.

He reached the willow trees that separated the plantation from Patrick's property and Glazer stood under them for a moment, surveying things. Neither Patrick nor his family was in sight and all the workers were gone.

Glazer followed the willow trees to the road, crossed, and found his holster near the tree. He pulled out the Colt and checked to make sure it was loaded. He pulled up his pant leg and slipped the revolver into his right boot. After making sure no one had seen him, he headed for Patrick's house.

The pump sat several yards behind the house, next to a trough and a small shed. Once the water was clear and flowing he took off his shirt, set it to one side, and ran his head under the water. He dug into his scalp with his hands, his fingers scrubbing away the dirt and sweat and pieces of cotton.

"My momma said to bring you this," a girl's voice said.

Glazer lifted his head from under the pump and wiped the water out of his eyes. One of the Doyle daughters, the youngest one, stood a few feet from him, holding a rough bar of soap in one hand. It smelled bitter and strong. The girl's mother stood behind her, in the doorway of the house. The little girl had her mother's eyes, her delicate ears. The mother smiled at Glazer. "Ma'am," he said.

"Did you work with my poppa?" the girl asked as she handed Glazer the soap.

"Yes." He took the soap and nodded at the little girl. "Thank you." He pumped the handle a couple more times then held the soap under the water for a moment before moving it across his chest and arms. The smell of it burned his eyes and nose.

"Sometimes my sister and I help. We carry weeds. He won't let us use any of the hoes or rakes. Says we're too young."

"He's just trying to keep you from getting hurt." Glazer handed the soap back to the little girl. "You give this back to your mother."

"Are you having supper with us?"

"That was the deal." Glazer went under the pump, the cold water rinsing away the soap. He briefly scrubbed his face before standing, water dripping off him.

"Were you shot?" the little girl asked. She pointed to the scars on his chest.

"Dolly," the wife said. "That's rude. Apologize."

"It's all right," Glazer said. He looked at Dolly. "I was shot by a cannon. It's something of a miracle that I'm even standing here. Not everyone was so lucky."

"Yes, sir. I'm sorry if I spoke out of turn."

"You're just curious is all. That's a good trait to have. There's no reason to apologize." Glazer flicked the water off his chest with his hands and shook his arms. He picked up his shirt and put it on. It felt filthy next his clean skin.

Patrick came around the side of the house. "You washed up?"

"Yes, sir."

"All right then, let's eat." He walked toward the house and as he did so, he picked up his daughter and tickled her on the stomach. She giggled.

Patrick's wife let them in and held the door for Glazer. After taking a last look at the setting sun, he went in.

"My name is Hannah," the wife said.

"Pleasure, ma'am. I'm Samuel."

She led Glazer through a small, clean kitchen and into the dining room. Patrick and the two girls were already seated at the table. Patrick motioned for Glazer to sit opposite the girls. A plate of chopped liver and a plate of grilled potatoes sat on the table. Glazer and Hannah took their seats.

"Let us pray," Patrick said. They joined hands and the family lowered their heads and closed their eyes. Glazer stared at them, each in turn. Hannah and the girls were so clean, so pretty. Their dresses new, full of color. He looked at Patrick, at the peace on the man's face, at his hands. The knuckles were red from work, the skin clean. Cleaner than it deserved to be.

"Dear Lord," Patrick said, "we thank you for your bounty and for allowing us to earn our way in this world. We pray for the souls of the fallen, for those that made the ultimate sacrifice in the pursuit of freedom. Please show them mercy and grant them entrance to your paradise. Please forgive us of our sins. Amen."

The girls repeated the amen and Hannah picked up the potatoes, scooped some onto the girls' plates, then handed the plate to Patrick. He dumped some onto his plate and passed it along to Glazer.

"How long were you in the army?" Patrick asked.

"About three years, give or take." Glazer slid off some of the potatoes and placed the plate next to Hannah. She was giving the girls some of the liver.

"I was in for two. By the end I was all the way up in Virginia."

"You ever wounded?"

"No. I take it you were." He gestured to the scar on Glazer's forehead.

"He was shot in the stomach, too," Dolly said. She smiled at Glazer as if the two of them shared a secret.

"That true?" Patrick asked.

"Got hit by some grape. None of it penetrated too deep."

"You're lucky. I saw lots of boys get blown to hell by that stuff."

"I don't want the girls hearing this," Hannah said.

"I'm not ashamed of what happened," Patrick said. "They need to know what we were fighting for. It's their heritage."

Hannah looked down at her plate, a scowl on her face. Glazer looked at her. She reminded him of the woman in the ad. They both had thin faces, long hair. Soft hair that would blow off their faces when the wind was right.

"You're originally from Missouri?" Patrick asked.

"That's right."

"What brings you down this way?"

"I stayed after the war ended. I had no reason to go back."

"No family?" Hannah asked.

"No, ma'am."

"I'm sorry to hear that," she said.

"Sometimes the fates have other plans for us," Glazer said. He looked at her and she held his eyes for a moment before turning away.

"I was up in Missouri once," Patrick said. He looked down at his plate, putting one piece of potato after another into his mouth. "Beautiful country."

"That it is." Glazer took a bite of the liver, which had been cooked in butter and lightly flavored with pepper. He chewed it slowly. "What were you doing up there?"

"Just visiting some friends. Nothing important."

"Nothing important."

"That's what I said."

"Stay for a while, did you?"

"Couple months, maybe a little longer."

"You get around much while you were up there?"

"Here and there. You know how it is."

"While you were traveling here and there, you happen to make it to a town called Fayette?"

"I don't think so." Patrick stopped eating and looked at Glazer.

"You sure about that?"

"I'm sure I'd remember if I had been there. I have a mind for such things."

"It was a small town," Glazer said. "The kind that's easy to forget. Think on it a bit, maybe you'll remember."

"I don't think I like your tone, mister. Lest you forget, you are a guest in this home."

"Patrick," Hannah said. "I'm sure he doesn't mean anything by it."

"He comes in off the road, and I show him the kindness the good Lord instructed and this —"

Glazer cut Patrick off. "You ever tell Hannah and your girls what you did while you were up there in Missouri? You and those friends of yours?"

Doyle pushed himself back from the table. "I think it's time for you to get the hell out of my house."

"You want to know why I don't have a family," Glazer said to Hannah. "Because your husband murdered them. Him and his friends. The brutality of it, I can't even begin to explain."

"That's enough!" Patrick got up and went for the shotgun mounted on the wall. Glazer pulled the Colt out of his boot and fired, the bullet striking the wood near the shotgun. Patrick stopped but did not turn around.

"Sit down," Glazer said.

Patrick turned and looked at Glazer. "If you think I'm going to just stand by and let you threaten my family—"

Glazer shot him in the left side of the chest, right below the clavicle. He fell back against the wall and slid down until he sat. He put his right hand over the bullet wound and blood spilled through his fingers. The girls both screamed and ran to their mother. Glazer kept the gun trained on Patrick.

"Why are you doing this?" Hannah asked.

"I found my wife hanging in the barn," Glazer said, his eyes locked onto Doyle. "They strung her up from the rafters. They burned her. All of her. Her skin was peeling off. I can still smell her." He looked at Hannah. "My boy was around back. They shot him three times, twice point-blank. Imagine seeing such a sight, imagine seeing your girls shot all to hell."

Patrick struggled to get up off the floor but only moved an inch or two before he fell back down. He coughed and flecks of blood stained his lips. "I'm going to kill you," he said.

"You need to tell your family what you really are," Glazer said. He stood and walked over to Hannah and pressed the gun against her head. She closed her eyes, tears rolling down her cheeks. "Go on, tell them."

"I'm not saying a damned word," Patrick said. His eyes were slits, focused on Glazer.

"Tell them how you rode with Bloody Bill. How you bastards went from one town to the next, doing whatever the hell you pleased."

"I will not."

"Confess or I swear to God that I will shoot your wife and daughters right here and now." Glazer pulled back the hammer on the pistol.

"Please," Hannah said, her voice barely a whisper. The girls whimpered in her arms. "Please don't do this."

"Tell them!" Glazer pressed down harder.

"You bastard," Patrick said. He looked at his wife. "I'm so sorry, Hannah."

Hannah looked at her husband, tears running down her face.

"Tell them you killed women and children," Glazer said.

"It's true," Patrick said, his voice deflated.

"Tell them what you did."

"I killed women and children. Some men too."

"And why'd you kill the men?"

"Because they got in our way."

"Because they got in your way."

"Let them go, this doesn't concern them."

"You're right, it doesn't." Glazer lifted the gun off of Hannah and walked over to Patrick. "Get up." Doyle struggled to get to his feet, his boots slipping on the blood that had pooled on the wood floor. Glazer grabbed him with one hand and steadied him and pushed him toward the front door. He stopped at the door and looked back at his wife, his eyes glassy and unfocused. Hannah wiped her eyes and looked at her husband. Glazer grabbed him and tossed him out of the house. Patrick lost his balance and tumbled off the front of the porch. Glazer turned and returned to the table.

"Do you have a pantry?" he asked Hannah.

"Please, I'm begging you, don't hurt my babies."

"Answer the question."

"It's off the kitchen."

"There a window in there?"

"No." She pulled her sobbing daughters closer.

"Get up," Glazer said.

Hannah stood, her arms still around her girls. "What are you going to do?"

"You know what I'm going to do. Now head for the pantry."

Hannah led the girls across the house and stopped in front of the pantry door. The girls clung to Hannah's legs. Glazer opened the door to the pantry. The inside was small and dark, shelves on three walls, each neatly packed with fruits and vegetables that were sealed in glass jars.

"Get in," Glazer said.

Tears rolled down Hannah's face and beads of sweat ringed her forehead, near the hairline. "Let the girls go, please."

"I'm not going to repeat myself," Glazer said. He gestured with the pistol.

Hannah led her girls into the pantry. "It's going to be all right," she whispered. "It's going to be all right."

Glazer shut the door and flipped the latch. He walked back into the dining room, knocked the plates off the table, flipped it over, and dragged it into the kitchen, pushing it against the pantry door.

From inside the pantry came the wailing of the girls.

He walked back into the dining room, took down the lanterns, and dumped their kerosene all around the house. He smashed one of the lanterns against the dining room table and the kerosene splattered across the table and onto the pantry door. He pulled a piece of burning wood from the stove and tossed it onto the table. The kerosene ignited.

As the fire roared to life, Glazer walked back through the house and went out the front door. Two black men stood near Patrick, one of them pulling him away from the house. The other held a shovel, wielding it like a weapon. Glazer aimed the pistol at them and both men backed away. Glazer walked over to Patrick and put his arms under his shoulders and sat him up.

"I want you to watch this," Glazer said.

"For the love of God," Patrick whispered, his throat dry and raw.

"The first two men, I just killed them. Walked up and shot them in the face and left their families alone. But right away I knew that it wasn't enough. I could feel it. And that's when I figured things out. It's about pain. Suffering. It's the only way he'll be satisfied."

"Who — who'll be satisfied?"

"You'll find out soon enough."

There was a loud pop from inside the house as more kerosene caught fire. Smoke billowed out the front door. Burning embers drifted up, carried by the heat. Two windows on the side of the house shattered from the heat.

"Your wife and daughters are burning," Glazer said. "Those pretty dresses, that clean, combed hair. All of it. That's your legacy. That's what you'll carry with you for the rest of your life." Glazer watched the burning house and breathed in the smoke, the heat. Patrick started to cough and Glazer knocked him to the ground. He took one last look at the house and walked away, the heat of the fire on his back, the sound of Patrick's choked wailing following him into the darkness.

MONDAY

1.

Kate carried the dirty laundry out of the bedroom and into the kitchen. She placed the laundry on the floor and got the soap down from the shelf above the stove. The soap was nearly gone, nothing but a thin bar, and she felt the edges with her fingers. It was going to have to do. She'd find a way to make it last.

After sorting the laundry, she took the least-soiled clothes outside and placed them on a small wooden table behind the house. She went back inside, got a large pot of warm water off the stove, and carried it out and placed it on the ground near the table. She grabbed a small stool and washboard, sat down next to the pot, and started to wash.

Jeremiah was tending to the chickens and when he saw that his mother was washing clothes he finished what he was doing and walked over to her. Kate finished scrubbing a pair of pants, rinsed them in a large pot filled with cold water, and handed them to Jeremiah. He took the pants over to the clothesline and hung them up, water running down the pants and dripping to the ground below.

"I'm sorry about yesterday," Kate said. She dunked a shirt into the warm water and ran it across the washboard, pressing it down hard against the metal. She scrubbed a spot of dirt and grease with a piece of soap.

"I don't understand why everyone was so mad."

"It's hard to explain."

"William beats his sister all the time. She showed me. He hits her across the back with an old strap."

Kate closed her eyes for a moment and took a deep breath. "They're going through a hard time right now."

"Because their poppa died in the war?"

"Yes." She scrubbed a shirt with the soap.

"He shouldn't hit his sister."

"No, he shouldn't." She rinsed the shirt and handed it to Jeremiah.

"Are we still going to see Uncle Emory?"

"Why wouldn't we?"

"He didn't say anything when he brought us home. Usually he's cracking jokes, swearing about people. It seemed like he's mad at us."

"He's not mad at us."

"I'll be glad when Poppa gets home."

Kate stopped washing and stared down at the soapy, brown water. A small eddy spun in the middle of the dark water, its centrifugal force pulling long strings of dirt down into the depths of the pot. Her eyes burned from anger. You've done this before, she told herself. You don't need anyone's help.

"You all right, Momma?"

"I'm fine."

"Are you sure?"

"That's enough, Jeremiah."

"Yes, ma'am." Jeremiah took a shirt from the rinse bucket and hung it on the line. Water ran down his arms and across his chest.

She rubbed a pair of pants hard against the washboard, trying to work out a grass stain. She rubbed the pants faster and faster and when she couldn't get them clean, she lifted the pants and dug into the stain with a nail, scraping and digging, scraping and digging, determined to get that green smear out of the cloth. Her nail split and she kept going, blood running down from the end of her finger.

"Momma?"

Kate raised her head and looked at her son. He stood next to her, his eyes wide. She looked down at her finger, at the blood smeared across the pants. She lifted her finger and put it in her mouth.

"You're bleeding."

"It's nothing. I just broke a nail." She got up and went into the house and leaned against the kitchen table, trembling. A thin stream of tears ran down her face. She picked up a hand cloth from the table and cried into it, the tears coming so thick and heavy that they erased her view of the world.

§

They were folding the dried laundry when Paul walked up to the back of the house. He had on the same dirty pair of overalls he always wore, no shirt underneath, his hair slick with sweat. He stopped when he reached the table and tipped his head toward Kate. "Hey there, Kate."

"Paul," she said as she folded. "What brings you out here?" She used a flat rock to keep the folded clothes in place.

"Heard about Lee, so I figured I'd come out and see if I could help."

"Well, we're all done with laundry," Kate said.

"I ain't very good at that. Besides, I meant over at the shop. Before he left, I told Lee I'd help him finish up some jobs, so if you don't mind I'd like to head over there for a couple of hours and see what I can get done."

"I can't pay you anything."

"I'm not doing a good job of explaining myself," he said. "I owe you money. This wouldn't erase any debt, but with things the way they are it's the least I can do. Maybe help bring in a little extra money for you two while Lee's gone."

"That's very kind of you."

"Lee's helped me through some tough scrapes. It's the least I can do."

Kate put down the shirt she was folding. "Jeremiah can go with you. He knows his way around in there and can show you where Lee keeps everything."

"I'm sure I could use the help. It's been a while since I've done any smithing."

"Let me get you the keys and a jug of water," Kate said. "It gets awful hot in there once everything's going." She walked into the house.

"You still have those cats?" Jeremiah asked. He sat down on the stool.

"Six or seven now. You want one?"

"Poppa won't let me."

"I'll talk to him when I get back. He could do with a good cat over at the shop, especially since he's always bitching about the birds. Cat would clear them out real quick." Paul spit. "All a dog does is lie around and shit all over the place."

Jeremiah laughed.

"He doesn't like cats because one of 'em pissed all over him when he was young." Paul winked at Jeremiah.

Kate came back outside and handed the keys and a large clay jug to Paul. "I keep this one under the floorboards so that it stays halfway cool. Jeremiah knows which key fits the lock."

"I'll have him back in time for supper," Paul said. He turned and started for the road, the jug hanging from one hand. Jeremiah glanced at his mother and ran to catch up with Paul.

2.

Eli had taken some of the jewels, enough to fill a side pocket on one of his panniers, but his brother had ignored the plunder, focusing instead on the two horses that belonged to the Union soldiers. He had given the stronger one to Lee and taken the gear off the other one and set it loose. At first it had wandered the field, unsure of what to do, but after a few minutes it bolted down the side of the road, heading north. Bobby had stood near the wagon and watched it go. Once it was out of sight, he tossed its saddle and bridle into the back of the wagon and pulled the drapery back over the bodies.

The three of them had ridden through the night, Bobby and Eli following behind Lee, and it was now just past midday, the sun hot and unrelenting. Patches of dark clouds rolled by, but none of them coalesced into anything. Lee had forgotten what it was like to ride day after day, how everything blended together until every new mile looked the same as the mile that preceded it. The fields around them were largely barren, the soil stripped of its nutrients by too many cotton plantings. Every so often there was a cluster of life in a small area where the soil still held some value, the plants clinging to it like it was an oasis.

The road dropped down a small hill. As Lee neared a curve at the bottom of the hill, a group of panicked women and children ran out onto the road. They were covered in dirt and bits of leaves. One of the women looked back at Lee and screamed. A cannonball sailed over Lee's head and crashed into the ground behind the woman. The force of it threw her into the air, her shattered arms and legs pinwheeling wildly as she flew. The women scattered, running and panting, desperate to escape from the cannon fire.

More cannonballs plummeted from the sky, as heavy as rain. A cannonball hit one little boy and tore him in two.

Lee slapped his horse's flanks, brought it to a full gallop.

To his left a woman lay on the ground cradling the bleeding, headless torso of a little girl. The woman's right leg was gone at the hip and blood pooled out from the wound, but she paid it no mind, her face turned to the sky, wailing. Lee chased down a small boy and just as he reached down to pull the boy up onto the horse, water rushed in from all sides. The water, dark and thick as mud, rose up to the boy's knees, then his waist. Lee dug his heels into the horse, but it couldn't move. It was mired in the same disgusting water that had trapped the boy, who screamed as he began to drown. Lee looked down and saw that the water was nearly to his own throat and in that dark liquid he saw his reflection, eyes dead and gray. The water turned boiling hot and he felt it burn him as he was swallowed by it.

Lee jerked awake. His eyes struggled to focus and for a moment everything was blurry and bright. He blinked several times, trying to clear them.

"Something wrong with you?" Eli said.

Lee closed his eyes and kept them closed for a few seconds. When he opened them again, the world still didn't look right.

"You hear me? You having a fit?"

"I fell asleep," Lee said. "Was having a dream."

"You were jerking all over the goddamn place."

Lee pulled out his canteen and took a long drink of water. There was a strong, bitter taste in his mouth. He took another drink from the canteen and sloshed the water around in his mouth. The bitterness persisted. "Heat must've finally gotten to me."

"You ain't going to keel over, are you?"

"I'm all right." He dumped some water onto his face. "The last time I was in the saddle this long was after the war, when I was heading home. Took me almost three weeks."

"Where were you?"

"North Carolina." Lee closed his eyes again and rubbed his face. The dream still clung to him, refusing to dissipate. It had all been so vivid, so real. He cleared his throat and spit.

"Me and Bobby were in Alabama."

"Mobile?"

"Selma, fighting with General Forrest."

"Didn't Selma get overrun?"

"'Cause those stupid pricks on the line cut and ran. Me and Bobby stood and fought as long as we could, but once we heard Mr. Forrest was injured, we fell back to Marion. Not long after that word came down that the war was over. Still burns my ass we lost that town."

"Wouldn't have made any difference."

"It's a point of pride."

"You'd have died for no reason."

"Didn't know it was the end while it was happening. I would've gone to my rest believing that I was still making a difference. That would've been good enough for me."

The bitter taste in Lee's mouth started to fade. He licked his teeth and spit again. "We spent a couple days just sitting around our camp," he said, "then a lieutenant came around and told us to pack our stuff, said the war was over. Then a different lieutenant came around and said no one was going anywhere, that we had to stay and give an accounting of what was ours and what was the government's. Half the men took off and the other half stayed. I waited a day. No one seemed to have any idea what was happening, so I grabbed what I could and started for home."

"They force you to sign those papers?" Eli asked.

"We were supposed to, probably even take an oath, but I wasn't going to wait around. I'd been gone long enough. I just wanted to go home. Figured they knew where to find me."

"They said we had to sign before they'd cut us loose. Some Union boys came into camp, tried to order everyone around. I told them I wasn't putting my name on anything. I didn't sign no papers when this started and I sure as hell wasn't signing any because it had ended."

Lee took another drink from his canteen, gurgled the water for a moment, then spit it out. The three weeks it took him to return home were the longest of his life. There was so much upheaval, civilians and soldiers returning home only to learn that they had no home to return to. He slept in fields and old barns and burned-out houses. The last four days he had nothing to eat. When he finally made it back, covered in dried mud and stinking of sweat, suffering from dehydration, he collapsed to the kitchen floor and slept for two days. The blackness of that sleep was dark and absolute.

"What'd those Union fellas say to that?" Lee said.

"Not a damn thing. Like I said before, most people don't want to get shot, especially over whether or not someone put his mark on a worthless piece of paper." Eli looked at Lee and smiled, his brown teeth moist with spit. "Still, I wouldn't have minded one more tussle with those bastards, show them that just because the Confederacy was beat didn't mean I was."

§

An hour or so later they reached a plantation. The main house sat off from the road and to the south of the house was a row of scorched willow trees, the branches black and barren, the ground around the trees seared down to the soil. On the other side of the willow trees rested the smoldering ruins of a house. Smoke rose up from the gray, charcoaled remains and the air stunk of burnt wood. Black men and women worked near the incinerated willow trees, digging fire-lines with shovels, dumping dirt on any areas where flames threatened to return.

Eli slowed down, waiting for Lee to catch up. "Looks like he was here," Eli said.

"Looks like it," Lee said.

"C'mon," Eli said. He turned his horse off the road and headed for the house. Bobby and Lee followed. The front was quiet but as they approached a young boy came out the front door and looked at them before running back inside.

Eli dropped off his horse, tied it to a banister, and walked up the stairs and knocked. Lee dismounted and joined Eli on the porch. Bobby stayed back on his horse, riding it from one end of the porch to the other while watching the black men and women working near the willow trees.

An old woman opened the door. She wore a blue dress, her hair thin and gray, eyes red and swollen.

"What do you want," the woman said, her voice cracked as she spoke.

"We'd like to find out how that house burned down," Eli said.

"I don't see how any of this is your business," the old woman said.

"Forgive us, ma'am," Lee said. "We're tracking a man, a known murderer. We just want to know if he had anything to do with this."

"You the law?"

"I'm a sheriff."

"Where are you from?"

"Tennessee," Lee said. He paused. "Each of us fought in the war."

The woman looked past Lee, out toward the road as if she was trying to find something or someone. Lee watched her. Tears slid down her face, following a path laid out by her wrinkles. "He spent the day working in the fields," she finally said. "He claimed that he just wanted some supper. My foreman Patrick, he took the man to his house at the end of the day and while they were eating the man locked Patrick's wife and daughters in the pantry and set the house on fire."

"What happened to Patrick?" Eli asked.

"He was shot. He'll live, but what kind of a life could a man expect to have after something like this?" She blinked the tears. "Those two little girls, those poor, sweet girls. Lord have mercy on them."

"Yes, ma'am," Lee said.

"I want to speak to Patrick," Eli said.

"He's not in any condition for company."

"We've been tasked with bringing the man who did this to justice," Lee said.

"Bring him to justice? The man who did this doesn't deserve justice."

"Yes, ma'am."

"When we find him, we're killing him," Eli said flatly.

The old woman moved out of the doorway. "Patrick is in the back. I'll show you."

Eli and Lee followed the old woman into the house, which was dark and hot and sparsely furnished. There were pale outlines on the floor where furniture had once sat. All of the windows stood open, the thin curtains limp in the still air.

The old woman led them to a small bedroom, off of the kitchen. Two white women sat at the kitchen table and a black woman stood at a counter, washing blood-stained linens in a large ceramic bowl.

"He's in here," she said. She walked into the room and stood near the headboard. Patrick lay on top of the bed's sheets, wearing nothing but a pair of drawers, a sheet folded over the bottom part of his legs. His chest was wrapped tightly with linens and a small blotch of fresh blood on the left side of his chest slowly seeped through the linen, creating a red spiderweb as it was absorbed into the wrap's fibers. Sweat rolled down Doyle's face and the old woman bent over and placed her hand on his forehead. He opened his eyes. "These men have some questions for you."

Patrick turned his head. "Who are you?"

"They're the law," the old woman said. "They're pursuing the man who did this."

Patrick coughed, his throat cracking. "Dammit, get me some of that water." The old woman picked up a pitcher from the dresser and poured a glass of water and handed it to him. He drank slowly, wincing from the pain of lifting his head. "You saw the house?"

"Yes," Eli said.

"He shot me. I couldn't do anything."

"Nobody said otherwise," Eli said.

"He made me watch. Sat me up in the front yard and made me watch." He handed the empty glass back to the old woman.

"Did he tell you why he was doing this?" Lee asked.

"Said he knew me from Missouri," Patrick said. He coughed several times and the red blotch on the linen wrap grew. He closed his eyes. "I'd never seen him before in my life."

"When were you in Missouri?"

"During the war."

"What were you doing up there?"

Patrick looked at the old woman. "Leave us. I need to speak to these men in private." The old woman opened her mouth as if to speak but instead she let out a deep sigh and left the room.

"You know what I was doing up there," Patrick said to no one in particular.

"My brother and me," Eli said, "we did some guerrilla fighting."

"The man who did this, he told me he fought with the Missouri Guards. Said his name was Samuel something-or-other."

"Up in Missouri, that was with William Anderson, right?" Eli asked.

"You heard of him?" Patrick said.

"Heard how they paraded him around after they murdered him. That's no way to treat a man."

"No, sir, it was not. Especially a man of his ilk."

"Why did Samuel kill your family?" Lee asked.

Patrick's face hardened and his mouth turned into a narrow slit. He glared at Lee.

"Because me and the men I was with killed his wife and son. Or so he claims."

"Was he telling the truth?"

"Anyone who got in our way, tried to keep us from doing what God put us on this earth to do, we cut them down. Man, woman, child, didn't make a whit of difference. It's why Anderson asked us to join up with him a short time later."

Lee fought back the urge to condemn Patrick's actions, to ask him how he could justify what he had done during the war. But it wouldn't serve any purpose. Men such as this were who they were. A man who took pride in murder would never see themselves for what they really were. "Was Samuel there?"

"No. Just the woman and boy."

"Then how'd he know how to find you?" Eli asked.

"I don't know. Maybe one of the other men got liquored up, ran his mouth, and word got out. But that doesn't line up. Too much time had passed."

"You know a man named Harold Camp?" Lee asked.

"He rode with us for a few months before he went off to Kansas. Hell of a man."

"His family was murdered a week or so ago. Same as yours. We tracked Samuel to another farm north of here, near a swamp. Looks like he was killed as well."

"That'd be Harlan Prescott," Patrick said. "He lost his family to yellow fever. That was the last time I heard from him."

"How many men were with you?"

"Out there at that farm? There were eight of us."

"And he's found at least three of you."

"The men you rode with, any of them live around here?" Eli asked.

"Nathaniel Keller was raised to the south of here, town called Rock Spring, but he was killed during the war. Squirrely son of a bitch, half the time he ran around wearing nothing but his drawers. Don't know if his momma's still around. Only other one is Matthew Abbott. Before the war he ran a plantation to the west of Atlanta. He might've gone back there once the fighting was over, but I can't say for certain."

Eli looked at Lee and the two of them turned for the door. "Sorry again about your missus and children," Lee said.

Patrick struggled up, his breath coming out fast and shallow. "You find this man, you gut him. Hear? Make him pay for what he's done."

"We will," Eli said. "You have my word on that."

Lee and Eli walked back through the house, the black woman following them. Eli went out the door and Lee slowed, keeping his eyes on the door, not looking at the woman.

"There's a man north of here," he said, "off in the woods at a camp of some kind, probably built by freed slaves. He's one of yours. You'll see to it?"

"Thank you, sir. I'll be sure to take care of that for you."

She held the front door open, Lee went outside and walked over to his horse. Eli was already in his saddle. Lee climbed onto his horse, which snorted and tossed its head from side to side. He dug his boots into its sides and tightened the reins, pulling the bit to the rear of its mouth. The horse quieted and started to trot, making for the road.

They went past the remains of the house at a full gallop. Two black men stood in the middle of the rubble and ash, shovels digging through the destruction in a final bid to uncover what was buried below.

3.

Paul stood next to the forge, sweat rolling down his face. The heat in the shop was excruciating, worse than he could have imagined. He ran the back of a gloved hand over his eyes and forehead, the leather smearing the sweat across his face. "Hand me that water," he said to Jeremiah.

Jeremiah walked over with the jug and gave it to Paul. Paul guzzled the last of the water. He panted, trying to catch his breath against the heat.

"That's it for today," Paul said. "Feel like I'm going to die." He reached up and reduced the airflow to the forge. "How long does it take for this to wind down?"

"Twenty minutes or so," Jeremiah said. "Poppa turns it down slow because he doesn't want to damage the chimney."

"Whole damned thing looks like it's about ready to fall apart. That pump around the back still work?"

"I'll show you."

Paul pulled off the gloves, placed them on the woodpile, and followed Jeremiah. He handed the jug to Jeremiah and went to work on the pump, moving the handle up and down until water started to flow. He stuck his head under the pump and soaked his hair down to the skin. Water ran down his back. After pumping the handle a couple of more times, Paul took a long drink. He took the jug from Jeremiah, filled it, and handed it back. "You better have some of this. Don't want you getting sick."

Jeremiah drank. Paul leaned against the pump, still fighting to catch his breath. Water trickled down from his hair and dripped onto his chest. "I don't know how your old man does it," he said. "Working in that sweatbox."

"He says it beats what he went through during the war," Jeremiah said, "that he has no right to complain."

"That is God's honest truth." Paul ran his fingers through his hair and wiped the water from his forehead. "I'm just not used to that heat."

"He used to throw up sometimes."

"I about lost it a few times myself." Paul closed his eyes and took deep breaths. He felt the water inside of him, spreading out from his center and cooling him.

Jeremiah sat down on an old tree stump and sipped from the jug. His shirt was soaked through with sweat. "You fought in the war with my poppa?"

"Part of the time, yeah. Let me see that jug." Jeremiah handed it back and Paul drank. He sloshed some of the water around the inside of his mouth before spitting it out. "The last year or so we got sent off in different directions."

"He never talks about it."

"It was a hard thing to go through. You have to take all of the things that make you who you are and bury them down deep, forget about them, because none of that'll help you."

"Did you kill a lot of people?"

"I suppose," Paul said. "Never had much of a choice."

"What was it like?"

"I don't think we should be talking about this."

"I mean did you feel sad about it?"

"Not at the time, but looking back ... hell, who knows. Those men didn't want to die any more than I did. But that's the only way such things are decided."

"I don't like the idea of my poppa killing people."

"It's not something he did lightly."

"What if the men he killed had children?"

"That's something you can't worry about." Paul looked down at the ground and pinched the water from his eyes. He took another drink from the jug. "A lot of it boiled down to dumb luck. You're out on post and you get up to take a leak and not three seconds later a cannonball comes flying in and the spot where you were just standing is blown to hell. You're still alive because you had to piss. Not sure what that says about the universe."

"Were you scared?"

"I did everything that was asked of me. And so did your old man."

"Momma was convinced Poppa wasn't going to make it," Jeremiah said, "that he was going to get killed right when the war was finally ending."

Paul looked at Jeremiah. How old had he been when Lee left? Four? Five? Too damned young to face something like losing your father. And yet here he was again, enduring the same trial all over again, worried about his father and wondering if he was going to come home a second time. "He talked about you, you know," Paul said. "Read me the letters from your momma. When he was done with them, he'd put them back in their envelope and wrap them in a brown piece of paper he carried with him. He saved every one of those letters."

"He only wrote us once."

"Shit, he wrote more than that. I sat there and watched him, sometimes I'd even hold a candle so he could see. But getting letters in and out of those places, well, that's another story. If the guy hauling the mail gets killed or captured, that's the end of that."

"Yes, sir." Jeremiah stared at the ground.

"Don't worry about your father," Paul said. "He's still the same man as before. And he'll be back before you know it." Paul took another drink from the jug. "All right, we better get this finished up. I'll check on the chimney if you want to get the sledgehammer and the splitter. We need to replace the wood that we used."

Jeremiah headed back into the shop. Paul watched him and sincerely hoped he hadn't just lied to the boy. He turned to the pump and refilled the jug.

4.

Kate sat at the kitchen table, slicing potatoes. They were undersized, not fully grown, but she wanted to grab them while she still could — more and more people were scavenging from the field down the road. She dropped the pieces into a small bowl and picked up the next potato, covered in dirt and small, immature roots extended out from the tuber, and washed it in a bowl filled with dirty water. She scrubbed it and plucked the roots, placing them on an old rag. The chickens would eat them.

From outside came the rattling of chains and an axle. Kate placed the last of the potatoes in the burlap sack and tied it off with a piece of string. The sound stopped near the back door. She wiped her hands on her apron and went outside.

Hansford climbed down from his carriage and smiled when he saw Kate standing in the doorway. A black man sat at the front of the carriage, staring off into space.

"I told you I wanted you off my property," Kate said. "And I meant it."

"Hello, Kate," Hansford said, his plump face flushed red. "It's dreadfully hot. Perhaps you'd invite me in for some tea."

Kate laughed.

"You find all of this amusing?" Hansford asked.

"Actually, I do," Kate said. "You know you're not welcome here and yet you have the temerity to walk up to my door and invite yourself in for some tea."

"I simply refuse to take no for an answer." Hansford walked over to the back door and stopped within a couple of feet of Kate. "I don't believe that your sentiment is genuine."

"Believe me, it is."

"For some people, Kate, life is like a hedge maze. They wander through its corridors day after day, lost and staying lost, unable to see what they want or how they are going to get it. I do not share that view of the world. I force my way through. I create my own corridors. Do you understand what I'm telling you?"

"I understand perfectly."

"We all have our God-given rights, Kate. I am merely exercising mine."

"Get the hell out of here."

Hansford moved close to Kate. "I tire of this, Kate. I've tried to be patient, to be a gentleman."

"I'm tired of this too." Kate stared at Hansford. She thought about taking a step back, but she was done giving ground. Anger swelled up inside of her. "Tired of you coming around here, strutting around like a damned peacock. What are you going to do that you haven't already done?"

Hansford smiled, stretching his mustache across his face. He leaned in closer to Kate. "Why do you think I sent Lee away with those two men?"

"To get him away from here."

"That's part of it, yes. The two men he's with are under strict orders to send me a telegram within the next two days. That telegram will ask a simple question and I will provide an even simpler answer, an answer that determines whether or not Lee will ever see this place again."

Kate struck Hansford across the face.

Hansford's smile vanished. He touched his face with two fingers. "It's time for you and Jeremiah to pack your things."

"We're not going anywhere. If you come out here again," Kate said, her bottom lip trembling from rage, "I'll kill you. I'll shoot you dead where you stand."

"As you wish." He looked at his fingers as if he expected to find something on them. Then he looked at Kate. "Within the next two days you will become a widow. Your son will have no father. The shop will be razed to the ground and when you are unable to pay the taxes on this land, the government in Washington will seize it."

"Get away from me," Kate hissed.

"We'll speak again soon." Hansford turned and walked to the carriage and climbed in the back. Kate stood motionless and watched as it returned to the road, her body shaking, tears rimming her eyes.

Once the carriage was out of sight, Kate went inside and walked to her bedroom. She opened the top drawer of the bureau and pulled out the pistol that Emory had given her. She loaded it with rounds from the brown paper sack. The pistol was surprisingly light, even when it was fully loaded.

She put the pistol and the bag of bullets on top of the bureau and walked over to the bed, bent down, and pulled out a shotgun and small wooden box. She checked to ensure the shotgun was loaded, then placed it on the bed next to the small box. Inside the box were fifteen shotgun shells.

She stood there, looking down at the shotgun. Such a simple thing, a piece of carved wood and some metal. When she was ten, her father Waylon had been killed by a shotgun during a firefight with moonshiners who had hidden their still on the family's property. When Waylon found the still he smashed it to pieces, tossing what was left into the creek. He was a man of faith who wouldn't tolerate a drop of alcohol in his presence, let alone on his land.

The moonshiners retaliated a week later, in the middle of the night. Kate awoke to an eruption of gunfire from the back of the house that seemed to go on and on and on. She heard her father yell something and there was more shooting. Then everything fell silent and the only sound was the wailing of Kate's mother.

She found her mother crouched over her father, who had been shot twice in the chest. Evidence of the buckshot that killed him littered his chest and neck and blood seeped from a hundred tiny wounds. Outside the back door were the bodies of three moonshiners. The nearest one still clutched a shotgun, the barrel smoking.

Kate sat on the edge of the bed and picked up the shotgun. She didn't know if Hansford was bluffing, but it didn't matter. There was nothing she could do. Kate simply had to trust that Lee would be able to deal with whatever came his way, trust that he would return to her once again. In the meantime, she'd have to be prepared for when Hansford returned.

5.

Glazer reached Rock Spring an hour before dark. It had rained earlier and the road was littered with puddles, the water brown and murky. A man and a woman, both dressed in tattered clothing, small bundles on their backs, walked down the side of the road, carving out a haphazard path to avoid the worst of the mud. Glazer overtook the pair and passed them by. Neither of them looked up.

Several empty buildings lined the road, the window frames dark and empty, the walls bending and sagging like melted wax. Rooftops collapsing from rot. The few standing buildings housed businesses. A dry goods store, a clothier for women called Molly's, a feed store, a tavern. Two old dogs sat in front of the feed store, both resting on filthy blankets.

At the town's only intersection, he turned east. The buildings on this road were intact but empty, the interiors dark and silent. On the edge of town was a three-story hotel and a livery. Two wagons sat in front of the hotel and from inside came the sounds of singing and clinking from an out-of-tune piano.

Glazer continued on. Across from the hotel, separated by overgrown railroad tracks, was a train station and a telegraph office. The station was abandoned, but the window for the telegraph office was open. An old man sat sleeping in the office, next to the window, his mouth hanging open. A cat lay sprawled out on the counter in front of the old man, its body pressed against the bars of the service window.

Five miles down the road was a long, short house surrounded by a ruined picket fence, the wood gray and battered. The west side of the house had collapsed, the roof running down to the ground like a ramp. Dirt had migrated up the slant and nearly half of the roof was covered with hundreds of flowers.

The paint was thin and nearly gone. The windows were covered with so much filth that they were no longer transparent. Along the front of the house ran a porch and an old woman sat on the far end in a rocker. She wore a large straw hat. Glazer rode past.

Once he was further down the road he stopped and looked back. Shadows covered much of the porch, but Glazer still saw the old woman, rocking back and forth.

From this vantage point he took in the rest of the property. Behind the house was a large stack of wood and a shed that looked ready to fall over. Just past that was an outhouse. Tall weeds grew everywhere, surrounding the shed and stack of wood. Only the outhouse was spared, the ground around it barren. Glazer guessed that the ground had been burned to keep anything from growing there. He turned his horse around and rode back to the house, stopping near the gate.

"Evening, ma'am," Glazer said. He turned his horse so that he directly faced the old woman. She continued to rock in the chair. Her dress was old and tattered and she wore an apron over the top of it that was so faded it was impossible to discern its original color.

"I heard you go past," she said. "I don't see much anymore, but my hearing's fine. Your horse has a little hop to its step, one-two-three, one-two-three, one-two-three." She clicked her mouth to the time of the horse's trot.

"Does a man named Nathaniel Keller live here?"

"I'm his momma," the old woman said. "Can you see the flowers on my roof?"

"Yes, ma'am."

"Pretty, ain't they? I'm blind in my left eye. Right eye's not far behind," she said, still rocking. "I planted those flowers up there before my left eye gave out on me. Spread seeds through the soil, watered them, put up bits of colored string to keep the birds away. They were just starting to come in when my left eye gave out. I can only barely see them even when the light's right, but I can smell them."

"They're lovely," Glazer said.

"My son is dead," the old woman said. "Killed up somewhere in Virginia. All I got for it was a letter I couldn't read. Had to have someone from town tell me what was marked on it."

"I'm sorry to hear that," Glazer said.

"I told him not to go. After his father died, God rest his soul, Nathaniel took to running all over creation. Drinking, whoring, you name it. Lost all respect for society. He'd be gone for weeks at a time. And when he did come back, he'd go and steal whatever wasn't nailed down before running off again. Cursed me, called me foul names. At a certain point I had to pull out my gun and warn him off, tell him he wasn't welcome here anymore. He said he was going to burn down my house but he never did. After that he stayed gone and here I sat. This is no way for a woman my age to live."

"No, ma'am."

"How did you know Nathaniel?"

"From the war. I just happened to be in the area and thought I'd look him up."

"You ain't one of those guerrillas?"

"No, ma'am."

"Good. If you're going to fight and kill, do it out in the open where everyone can see. Don't be a coward about it."

"Yes, ma'am. I fought with the regular army."

The old woman stopped rocking. "You're still on that horse of yours, ain't you?"

"I am."

"My name is Mary. If you help me with the wood, I'll make us something to eat. It's the least I can do since you've come all this way."

"I wouldn't want to impose," Glazer said. He looked at Mary, at her dead left eye. Even in the gathering gloom it looked unnatural, nearly luminescent.

"You'd be doing me a favor. I got some squirrel and a sweet potato and maybe a radish or two."

Glazer looked at the road then back at Mary. She struggled to get up from the rocking chair, her right arm shaking as it supported her weight. He thought about her son, but he couldn't tie the two of them together.

"If it's not going to be any trouble," Glazer said.

"Already told you it ain't. The axe is back by the wood. You can tie up that horse of yours near the shed. There's a water pail there." Mary slowly hobbled toward the front door and opened it. "When you're done, come in through the back. It's open."

Glazer climbed down and led his horse through the gate and around to the back. On one side of the shed was a water pail and after he secured his horse he walked over to the pump. He worked the handle for a couple of minutes before the water flowed, coming out dark and thick, stinking of mud and metal. He kept pumping the handle until it was clear. He rinsed the pail, filled it, and placed it under the horse's head. The horse ignored it.

The axe laid buried in some weeds near the wood. Glazer picked it up and wiped away the dirt and cobwebs, and ran a finger down the edge of the axe head. It was even duller than he thought it would be. He carried it over to the pump and washed it off, before walking back to the wood.

He didn't so much chop the wood as he did bludgeon it into pieces. Once he had a decent stack of small and splintered pieces, he dropped the axe, gathered up the wood, and went in through the back door.

The inside was nearly empty. The back door led directly to the kitchen and Glazer put the wood down near the stove. Mary stood at the table, cutting a sweet potato with a small knife. A skinned, gutted squirrel sat on the table, and she put the pieces of the potato next to it. There were no chairs. Glazer looked around. At the front of the house was one room that doubled as a bedroom and sitting room. Near the front door sat a ragged old couch and pushed against a far wall was a bed. The walls were bare, save for a framed picture of Jesus Christ that hung above the bed. The section of the house that had collapsed was visible through a door, and the wall on that side bowed out, the wood splintering in several places. Three dusty lanterns lit the house.

"I eat on the bed, if that's what you're wondering," Mary said. "Had to sell everything else."

"It's fine," Glazer said. "I've eaten in a lot worse places."

"I imagine that's true. You want to get that fire going? There's some matches on the window sill."

Glazer took the matches and started a fire inside the stove. He had to work the flue back and forth to get it loose before the flames finally took hold and even then smoke drifted back into the house.

"Chimney's half-clogged," Mary said.

"Gets any worse it might burn your house down."

"I rarely use it, only when I got company." She turned away from the table, took down a cast iron skillet that hung from one wall, and swept the squirrel and pieces of potato into the skillet. "Once it's hot, I'll put this on."

"I'm much obliged," Glazer said.

"Couldn't find that radish. I might've already ate it."

"It's fine." He tended to the fire, using an old poker to press the wood into the center of the stove. He closed the door to the stove and put the poker back into the tin can that held it.

"You're not from these parts, are you?" Mary asked.

"No, ma'am."

"You don't have that drawl in your voice. One-two-three, one-two-three." She started to whistle and placed the skillet on top of the stove. Within moments the skillet's seasoning sputtered to life.

Mary used a wooden spoon to flip the meat and the bits of potato. Grease popped and flared out of the skillet. Mary continued to whistle as she cooked and Glazer leaned against the wall and watched her. An old woman in an old house cooking her final meal.

"You can stay here tonight," Mary said. "Ain't no sense in riding around in the dark."

"That won't be necessary."

"I just sit out in that chair most nights, sleeping whenever it comes over me. You can have my bed if you want."

"I'll probably be going after supper."

Mary turned and looked at Glazer, her left eye glittering in the lantern light. "It's been a long time since I've had a man sleep under this roof."

Glazer looked at the squirrel frying in the skillet. There was no other food in the kitchen. That squirrel and potato was all she had and she was offering it to him.

"Let me get my things and turn out my horse," Glazer said. "I'll be right back."

§

He doesn't much believe in God but he goes to the revival anyway because his friend Roy says that women from all over the county will be there. He sits and listens to three preachers talk about Hell and the Devil and how to achieve atonement through the blood of Jesus Christ. It's hot in the tent and when the fourth preacher takes the stage, claiming to be a healer of an entire list of ailments, he gets up and walks outside. Roy's long gone, probably already shacked up with someone.

There are two other tents on the grounds, one of them selling food and the other offering religious items. Crosses, paintings, healing water, and small wood carvings of the saints. He buys some tea and then looks at the trinkets. The man working the booth tries to sell him some water that came from upstate New York but when he tells the man he doesn't have any money, the man moves on to someone else.

He sees her sitting by herself at a table under a large oak tree. She's reading a periodical and her hair is freshly washed and pulled loosely behind her. After a few moments of watching her, he decides to say hello. He figures that if she rejects him, he'll never have to see her again anyway, and if she doesn't, it'll give him something to do until Roy gets back.

He sits down across from her and says hello and she looks up and smiles. She has deep brown eyes. He asks her what she's reading and she shows him a copy of Putnam's Magazine. He's never heard of it. He asks her if she's enjoying the revival and she says she came with her sister, who wanted to be touched by the faith healer because there's something wrong with her legs. He doesn't know what to say to that, so he simply says he's sorry and she smiles at him and says that it's all right. We are made to be who we are and not even God can change something once the mold's been set.

They sit and talk until her sister comes out of the tent. She looks like she's been crying and she walks with a slight limp. She sits down next to her sister and says that the faith healer tried twice to rid her of her pain. He told her to come back again and in the meantime she needs to pray to Jesus for a miracle.

He thinks the sister is beautiful and he says so. The sister blushes and says that's very kind of him but he doesn't need to lie. He tells her he's not lying. She has brown hair and wears a pale yellow dress. She's younger than her sister by a year. He asks her how she was hurt and she says that she got kicked in the back by a calf a few years ago. Some days are better than others. He talks to the younger sister, the older one reading her periodical, until Roy returns, hair ruffled and grinning. He asks the younger sister if he can call on her and she looks embarrassed but she says yes. The one with the periodical smiles.

He watches them walk away. Roy laughs and says that he's too polite. Need to bust straight out of the gate at full speed if you want to get anywhere with a woman. He tells Roy to be quiet and Roy laughs. I got enough for the both of us, Roy says.

After that he sees the sister as often as he can, usually two or three times a month. Eventually her father asks when he's going to grow a pair and ask him for her hand in marriage. It's a love story like every other love story. Nothing remarkable except to those caught up in the middle of it, and in the years to come he realizes that she fills a void in his heart that he hadn't even known existed.

TUESDAY

1.

Glazer spent the night lying on the bed, staring at the ceiling. He was still fully clothed, boots and all. He thought about the old woman sitting out there, her son. About his wife and child. He got up, pulled his pistol out of its holster, and went out to the front porch. Mary was in her rocker, quietly whistling to herself. The back of her chair made a slight thumping sound as it struck the side of the house.

"I see my son sometimes," Mary said, not looking at Glazer. "He stands right there on the side of the road and stares at me. Usually his innards are hanging out, but other times there's just a clean bullet hole in the middle of his forehead."

Glazer stood next to her, facing the road, the pistol in the hand opposite of Mary, flush with his leg.

"He doesn't say a word. Just stands there and stares. Sometimes he opens the gate and wanders around the yard, like he's trying to find something. The first few times I got up and followed him, asked him what he was looking for, what he wanted. But he'd just turn and look at me and not say a word." Mary stopped rocking and looked at Glazer. "Why won't he talk to his momma? What kind of a God would put a mother through such torment?"

"I've often wondered that myself," Glazer said.

Mary stopped rocking and looked at Glazer. She turned away from him and resumed her rocking. "Who was it?"

"My wife and son."

"They killed during the war?"

"Yes." Glazer tightened his grip on the pistol.

"The tragedy of it all will overwhelm you if you let it. A loss like that." She sighed and stopped rocking, but she kept looking out at the road. "Men are savages. That's the God's honest truth. They'd tear up the whole damned world if they could, spilling blood just for the sport of it. Folks should be able to live without worrying about someone coming up behind them and cutting their throat."

"Yes, ma'am," Glazer said.

"I learned a long time ago that there's no peace in this life. Look at

167

me, living in this house. Half of it fallen down, the other half barely standing. I'm a widow, the mother of a dead son who shouldn't be mourned. The only thing that keeps me going, that puts a smile on my face, is the hope that once this is all said and done my soul will get some rest. That my grave will be warm and safe and comforting."

The two of them stayed silent, the sun slowly rising in the east. A rabbit ran out onto the road and sat in the warm sun for a moment. Then it was gone.

"I know what you are," Mary said, "why you're here. Knew it the second I heard you. One-two-three, one-two-three."

Glazer looked at her.

Mary's eyes turned wet. She turned and looked at Glazer. "Can I ask one thing of you?"

"What's that," he said.

"Can you give me this day? Let me check on the flowers, make sure they'll be all right. Then once the sun goes down, you can do whatever it is you need to do." Her dead eye looked at Glazer. "No one's ever given me much of anything, but if you give me this day, well, it'd help me get my soul ready for what's to follow."

Glazer fingered the trigger on the pistol and stared at the road. He tried to imagine Nathaniel standing out there, tormenting his mother even in death, guts dangling all over the place, swaying as he stumbled around.

"Yes, ma'am," he said.

Glazer took one last look at her sitting in her chair, rocking back and forth, quietly weeping, and went inside. He put his pistol in its holster, took off his boots, and lay down on the bed. Outside the birds started to sing with the rising sun and he wondered what it'd be like to know that the day facing you was your last.

2.

Lee sat up and rubbed his face and looked at the sky. He guessed it was an hour or so after sunrise. Bobby and Eli sat on opposite sides of the fire, the old coffee pot percolating on the metal meshing. Lee got up and walked over to the fire. His eyes hurt from a lack of sleep and his stomach burned with hunger. They had stopped well after midnight and the only thing to eat had been the last of the ham.

"You want some of this coffee?" Eli asked.

"Is it from last night?"

"Bobby finished that up. This is fresh."

"Yeah, all right." Lee picked up his cup off the ground, looked to make sure there was nothing crawling around inside of it, and waited for the coffee to get done.

"You tired?" Eli said.

"Aren't you?"

"No. Today's the day we finally catch that bastard. I can feel it." Eli picked up the coffee pot, filled his and Bobby's cups, then handed the pot to Lee. Lee poured his coffee and placed the pot back on the meshing.

"What happens if he's in the middle of town?" Lee blew on the coffee, his mind working on a way to get out of this, to break free from the brothers.

"Then he's in the middle of town."

"Back when I was sheriff, if three guys walked into my town and shot someone I'd sure as hell want to know about it beforehand. Otherwise I was liable to come out guns first."

"You think any of these pissant towns have any law worth a damn?"

"Maybe not the law as we think of it, but they'll have someone with a gun hanging around, just in case." Lee sipped the coffee. It was hot and bitter and helped settle his hunger pains. "Unless you're planning on shooting them, too."

"It won't come to that."

"If we're as close as you think we are, we should tell the locals."

"And what if this Samuel fella catches wind of what we're doing?"

"He doesn't know anyone around here."

"Maybe not, but if he sees folks running around, closing their shutters and locking their doors, he doesn't have to be a genius to figure out that something's happening."

"It could get ugly."

"Once that bastard is laid out, we'll just show folks that badge of yours. As long as we have it, doesn't matter what we do." Eli finished his coffee, grabbed the pot, and refilled his cup.

"I'd be pretty pissed."

"Well you're not the law around here."

"No, I'm not." Lee finished his coffee. He assumed that the brothers wouldn't move against him until they had dealt with Samuel, that they'd turn on him either during or after the confrontation. Once Lee was dead, Eli could make up some story, claim that Lee and Samuel were in cahoots. It wasn't like Lee's badge had a name on it.

Lee stood up, gathered his bedding and panniers, and carried them over to his horse. The horse snapped at him and he slapped it on the side to quiet it. Lee secured the panniers and slung the bedding across the back of the saddle. He looked toward the fire and Bobby still sat there, staring at him, the handkerchief that covered his face moving in and out to the tune of his breathing.

§

It took them nearly six hours to reach Rock Spring and they entered the town riding single file with Lee pinned between Bobby and Lee.

Lee examined the town, its ruin. The collapsing buildings, overgrown with weeds, the road permanently scarred with deep furrows from the never-ending weight of heavy military wagons. Had the citizens eagerly assisted the Confederate army when it came through and stripped the town of everything worth taking? And what had they thought on the day after, when the army was gone and the excitement had died off and the town was left with nothing? Lee had seen countless towns such as this and he knew that none of them would do anything differently if given the choice. They all believed that the Confederacy was going to win as firmly as they believed in God and because of that they were willing to pay any cost. Even if it meant unleashing a self-inflicted cataclysm.

In front of the feed store sat an old man and two young women. Lee nodded at them. The old man mouthed his gums but otherwise didn't move. The young women just stared, eyes wide and glassy.

They reached the town's intersection and turned east, Bobby still out in front, riding down the right side of the road. The road was empty and quiet. Lee reached the hotel on the eastern edge of town and Eli told him to stop. Bobby kept on, heading for the edge of town. Lee turned his horse around.

"I need to send a telegram," Eli said. He dropped off his horse and tied to the post in front of the hotel. "Wait here with the horses."

Lee looked across the tracks at the telegraph office. "Who are you sending a telegram to?"

"Who do you think?"

"Hansford."

"Yes, Hansford. Before we left he told me to send him an update once we were close to bringing all of this to an end."

"Where's your brother going?"

"To see how far ahead Samuel is. Stay here." Eli crossed the tracks.

Lee dismounted and tied his horse next to Eli's. He stepped up onto the porch of the hotel so that he could see Eli, who was bent down in front of the service window, speaking to an old man. The old man wrote on a piece of paper as Eli spoke and Eli handed him some money. The man started tapping the transmitter. A cat jumped up onto the counter and sat by his hands, watching the transmitter click up and down.

There was no sign of Bobby. Lee doubted he was actually looking for Samuel. More likely, he was hidden off to the side of the road somewhere in the weeds, watching Lee, waiting to see if he was going to do something. Lee thought about getting his Henry. He had a clean shot at Eli and could bring him down with a single bullet. But if Bobby was out there, the second shot fired would be the one that took Lee's life. He looked at the rough road and spit.

Eli came back to the hotel and climbed up the stairs to stand beside Lee. "Bobby's going to meet us here," Eli said. "Let's go inside, I'm tired of being out in this sun."

The inside of the hotel was dark and dusty, the doors and windows all open as far as they would go. A slight breeze swirled through the hotel's lobby but it wasn't enough to cut through the heat. On the wall opposite the door was a large wooden counter and on one side of the counter were a handful of tables and on the other a staircase that wound up to the second floor. An old, faded rug sat in the middle of the lobby and on top of it were two couches. A piano occupied the corner nearest the door.

A skinny young man stood behind the counter. He wore a white shirt and black suspenders and his red hair was split down the middle with a part.

His forehead was sprinkled with dandruff. Lee walked over to the counter while Eli sat down at one of the tables, his back to the wall.

"How can I help you?" the young man said.

"You serve food?" Lee asked.

"We've got catfish and potatoes. Costs one dollar even."

"That come with something to drink?"

"Yessir, either coffee or sun tea. Your choice."

"I'll have the tea."

"Yes, sir," the young man said. He disappeared through a side door. Lee sat down at a table next to Eli so that the two of them faced the same direction.

"Too good to sit with me?" Eli asked.

"Just want to be able to see who comes through the front door."

"Fair enough." Eli pulled out his pouch of chew and stuffed some into the side of his mouth. "You know when Bobby comes back, we're leaving. Probably shouldn't have ordered any food."

"I'll take my chances."

Eli looked around for a spittoon and found one in the corner. He went over and put it next to his table before sitting back down.

"What was that telegram about?" Lee asked.

"I told you, just updating Hansford."

"What'd you tell him?"

Eli spit into the spittoon. "The hell you think I told him?"

"Did he send a reply?"

"There was nothing to reply to. I sent him a statement, not a question." Eli spit again. "I'm tired of these shithole towns, you know? Once this is all over and done with, me and Bobby are lighting out for Texas. Decided last night."

The young man brought out the plate with several slices of breaded catfish, fried potatoes heaped on one side, and a tall glass of tea. He pulled a fork and cloth napkin from a pocket and placed them on the table next to the plate. He looked at Eli. "Did you want anything?"

"Did I ask for anything?"

"No, sir."

"Then what the hell makes you think I want something?"

The young man frowned and returned to the counter. He opened a ledger and started to write with a small pencil.

Lee ate his food. The catfish tasted delicious and it was obvious that whoever had cooked it knew how to get the mud out of it. Eli watched him eat, and when he was finished Lee stood up and walked over to the counter. "You have an outhouse?" he asked the young man.

"It's around the back," the young man said. "Go through this side door and follow the hallway. You'll see it once you get out there."

"Where are you going?" Eli said.

Lee looked at him. "To take a shit. You want to tag along?"

Eli spit.

Lee nodded his thanks to the clerk and went out through the side door and walked down the hallway. Before he stepped outside, he looked back to make sure that Eli wasn't following him. The hallway was empty. He opened the door and started for the telegraph office. As he walked, he pulled out his sheriff badge and pinned it to his chest.

"Busy day," the old man said as Lee approached. Most of the old man's teeth were gone and deep wrinkles crisscrossed his face.

"I'm down here tracking a couple of fugitives," Lee said. He pulled on his shirt so that the man could see his badge. The old man looked at it then took in Lee's face. "They might have come through here in the last few days and sent a telegram. You mind showing me copies of what you've sent and received?"

"Sure, sure," the old man said. He picked a folder off the floor and opened it. Inside were his handwritten notes, each scribbled out on pieces of yellow paper. He took out most of the paper and pushed it off to the side and sorted through the remaining notes. "I tend to write everything down. Can't trust these damn machines."

"Take your time." Lee looked back at the hotel.

"These are the ones from this week," the old man said. He shuffled through the notes, his hands lightly shaking. "Five sent and two received. Want me to read them to you?"

"How many were sent yesterday?"

"None."

"Today?"

"Two."

"I just need to hear those two." Lee turned so that his left side was against the service window. He lowered his head and watched the hotel out of the corner of his eye.

The old man lifted up the paper and squinted at his writing. "The first one says: 'My dearest mother. Stop. I'm afraid I have heartbreaking news. Stop. Eliza passed away two days ago. Stop. You were in her thoughts until the end. Stop. Love William. Stop.'" The old man looked at Lee. "I knew Eliza.

She was a decent woman. Heard it was the cancer that got her. Hell of a world we live in."

"What about the other one?" Lee continued to watch the hotel. A dog wandered around, sniffing the ground. It caught the scent of something, pressed its nose hard against the ground, and ran off.

"Just give me a second here." The old man lifted a different piece of paper and moved it closer to his face so he could read it. "Damned handwriting. All right, this one says: 'Nearing the end. Stop. What to do about Lee? Stop. Yes or no? Stop.'"

"Was there a response to that one?"

"It just said yes." The old man gathered up the papers and put them back into the folder. "That was no more than twenty or thirty minutes ago, I think the fella that sent it went over to the hotel." He dropped the folder onto the floor. "Either one of those what you're looking for?"

"No," Lee said. "Don't mean anything to me."

"Is this something we should be worried about? Things are finally getting back to normal around here and the last thing we need is for the place to get torn to shit. Pardon my language."

"Don't concern yourself with it. They didn't come this way," Lee said. "And even if they had they'd be long gone by now. I thank you for your help."

"Sure, sure," the old man said. He picked the cat up off the floor and stroked the top of its head. "You have yourself a nice day now."

"You too." Lee took a wide angle on the way back so that no one could see him approach from the front of the hotel. His best chance was to get Eli now, while he was alone.

He reached the back door and looked down the hallway. It was empty. He went into the outhouse and stood there, thinking. He checked his pistol to make sure it was loaded with clean rounds. He closed his eyes and drew in several deep breaths through his mouth. He was going to walk into the hotel and shoot Eli. Once Eli was dealt with, he'd wait for Bobby to return. He'd show his badge to the young man and tell him he could clear out if he wanted, but from the outside everything had to appear normal. He'd take up a position behind the counter and the moment Bobby came in through the front door he'd gun him down and that would be the end of this.

Lee reached for the door but stopped himself. Instead he went for the knife that hung off the back of his belt. He pulled it out of its sheath and slid it down the inside of his right boot, the handle up and within easy reach. Lee tightened his grip on his pistol and stepped out of the outhouse. He went in through the back door of the hotel and walked down the hallway. When he reached the lobby, he bent a bit and raised his gun and prepared to fire.

The tables were empty.

"How was your shit?" Eli asked, his voice above Lee.

"Fine," Lee said. He didn't move.

"Put your gun on that counter. That badge of yours, too."

Lee dove for the counter. The moment he moved, bullets slammed into the wood. Splinters filled the air, a pitcher of water shattered. Lee moved quickly down the length of the counter, head down but eyes up. He saw movement on the landing above and he raised his pistol and fired. All he hit was bannister.

"That my Henry?" Lee asked.

"Hell of a gun," Eli called down. "Got a nice balance to it." The rifle fired again. The bullet sailed over Lee's head and smashed into the mirror behind the counter. Pieces of the mirror and various liquor bottles rained down. Lee moved out of the path of the falling glass, toward the end of the counter. He looked toward the front door. Fifteen feet, maybe twenty, the only cover the piano.

Lee raised his pistol and fired. The bullet blew out part of a handrail and Eli moved toward the stairs, keeping his head low. Lee tracked him and fired again. He was at a significant disadvantage. Eventually Eli would find a position that negated the cover the counter provided. His only option was the front door. He fired again and ran for the piano. As he reached it, two bullets slammed into it. One of them took out most of the keys, the other plowed through the center of it. The strings broke, let out a high-pitched wail. Metal slapped wood. Lee moved around to the front of the piano, fired twice, and went for the door.

The bullet took him in the left leg, just above the knee, right in the meat of the thigh. Lee dropped to the floor, one hand on the bullet wound, the other still holding his pistol. He heard boots running down the stairs and he turned and raised the pistol. He had a clean shot. Lee pulled the trigger, but the firing pin hit nothing. Empty.

Eli crouched down next to Lee. There was a cut across the left side of Eli's throat. Blood dripped from it.

"Hansford was right about you," Eli said. He ran a finger across the cut. "Even with the handrail and all the uprights, you still almost got me."

"Fuck you," Lee said.

Eli smiled. He grabbed Lee's pistol, slid it across the room, and took the badge off of Lee's shirt. He put it in his pocket. He took Lee's right arm and ripped the shirt sleeve off at the shoulder. He pulled it off of Lee's arm and looked at the wound, his fingers pushing on the edges of both the entry and exit wounds.

"If you're going to kill me, kill me," Lee said.

Eli smiled. His brown teeth dripped with saliva. "I ain't gonna kill you. Not that I don't want to, mind. But I promised my brother. He's been thinking about it ever since we met you." Eli wrapped the cloth around Lee's wound and tied it tight so that it'd stop the bleeding.

Lee lay back and closed his eyes. His leg was a fountain of pain. Sweat dripped from his face.

"Been a shitter of a day, ain't it?" Eli said.

3.

Kate walked through the shop, looking to see if she had missed anything. Jeremiah watched her from the front door, the wheelbarrow at his side. He wore his father's leather work gloves. The wheelbarrow carried some tools that Lee had purchased after he rented the shop, the work that Paul and Jeremiah had completed, and other odds and ends. Things Kate didn't want to lose.

She looked through a large wooden toolbox that held all manner of implements and she pulled out two small hammers and showed them to Jeremiah. "Did your father buy these or did they come with the shop?"

"I think Poppa bought them."

"But you're not sure?"

"No, ma'am."

"Better leave them here, then," Kate said. "I don't want anyone accusing us of being thieves." She dropped the hammers back into the wooden toolbox.

"Does this mean we're never coming back here?" Jeremiah asked.

"Probably."

"Won't Poppa be mad?"

"You let me worry about him."

"Yes, ma'am." Jeremiah pulled at the gloves, making sure that they were on as far as they'd go. "I thought Mr. Guthrie liked poppa working here."

"He did, but he sold it to someone else."

"Did they kick Poppa out?"

"More or less." Kate turned in a circle, taking in the shop one last time. "All right," she said as she walked to the front of the shop. Jeremiah lifted the handles on the wheelbarrow and pushed it outside. He stopped and waited for his mother to lock the front doors. She ran the chain through the doors, placed the lock, and pulled on it to make sure it was secure. After taking one last look at the old building, she walked over to Jeremiah and the two of them started for home.

The return trip took them nearly an hour and by that time, Jeremiah was drenched in sweat. He pushed the wheelbarrow up to the back door and they unloaded it, putting everything on the back porch.

Kate brought out a glass of water and handed it to Jeremiah. He drank it all in one gulp.

"When Poppa comes back are we going to move?"

"Why do you ask that?"

"Because we don't have the shop anymore."

"I don't know."

"Can he do something else?"

"Not around here." Kate sat down on the back step.

"Uncle Emory knows a lot of people."

"He does, but none of those people have money."

"I was born here," Jeremiah said.

Kate looked at the glass, rolled it between her hands. "Sometimes things are beyond your control."

"You all right, Momma?"

"I'm fine," Kate said. She looked at him and forced a smile. "We've made it through worse than this."

"I remember when the only thing we ate was potato soup. It was runny and all you could taste was the salt. I hated every bite of it."

"You were so glad when we finally had some squash."

"I hate squash too."

Kate laughed. She had worked so hard to keep Jeremiah from fully understanding how dire their situation was when Lee was gone. She'd steal little bits of food — an onion or a carrot or a piece of jerky — and surprise Jeremiah with them. She told him that there was a secret stash of food hidden on their property that Lee had buried before he left. During the first year, Jeremiah would walk around with a shovel, trying to find it. Even when he got older and realized that any extras they had were a result of Kate scrounging and stealing, he still pretended to believe that the secret stash was out there.

"Can I tell you something," Kate said. "I hate squash, too. All those seeds disgust me. I hate it almost as much as zucchini."

"But you make zucchini all the time."

"Because your father loves it."

"Does he know you don't like it?"

"No, he thinks I like it as much as he does. But every bite makes me retch." He smiled at her.

Kate nodded. Across from them the chickens walked in their pen, scratching and pecking at the ground. She looked at the sky. Dark clouds gathered to the west and they were backlit by the sun, reds and yellows bursting out. The sky was a dark violet.

4.

Glazer knelt near his horse and cut its matted belly hair with a pair of old shears he'd gotten from Mary. The horse stood still and every few minutes he patted it on the side, just to let it know that everything was all right.

He tossed the shears to one side and picked up a large metal file and examined the horse's hooves, digging out any rocks or packed dirt that had become stuck. When he came to the hoof with the cracked horseshoe, he used the file to scrape back part of the hoof. Once he was done, he stood and turned the horse out, making sure that it had easy access to water. The horse sniffed the air and stood still.

Glazer gathered up the tools and went inside. He put them on the kitchen table and crossed the house and went out the front door. Mary sat in her chair, rocking back and forth, humming under her breath. Glazer sat down on an old tree stump that he'd brought around from the back.

"Get your horse cleaned up?" Mary asked.

"Yes, ma'am."

"We only ever had one horse, but it was beautiful. I believe that they're a gift from God."

Something moved in the woods across the road and Glazer pretended not to notice. It moved slow and steady and after seeing a flash of color, Glazer determined that it was a man. The man stayed behind the larger trees, using the growing shadows as cover, and he stopped near a trunk that was surrounded by thick ferns. The man held a Sharps but it wasn't raised. The man was just watching and so Glazer let him watch.

"Where are you from?" Mary asked.

"Missouri."

"I've never been up north. Will you ever go back?"

"No."

"I saw the Mississippi river once," Mary said. "I was a little girl and we were over in Louisiana visiting family on my father's side. I think it was my great-uncle. We crossed the river on a ferry and I remember the water being so dark and so deep. Seemed like it took forever to get across. On the way back we crossed at night and it felt like I was floating in the middle of nothing, like the entire world had disappeared. I lost all sense of time." Mary picked up a glass of water, her hand shaking, and took a drink. "That was the one and only time I left this county."

"My wife always wanted to see the ocean," Glazer said.

"I imagine there's nothing like it."

"I imagine not." The man in the woods stayed perfectly still. "The closest we ever came were some pictures in a book that I bought her in Kansas City."

"Neither one of us could read, but my husband liked the feel of books. He'd scrounge them up and if they had pictures in them, we'd look at them in the evening, before we went to bed. We'd laugh and joke about all the places we were going to see. He'd spin entire stories out of those pictures. That was his gift." Mary clicked her tongue off the roof of her mouth. "One-two-three, one-two-three, one-two-three."

"My son did the same thing."

"I miss my husband something terrible," Mary said. "The only thing that gets me through each day is the hope that he's waiting for me, that the love we had will carry us through all of eternity." She looked at Glazer. "Do you believe in such things?"

"No," Glazer said. He watched the man across the road. The man still held the Sharps rifle at his side, but if he was going to shoot, he already would have. The man was here to get the lay of things. He slowly backed away from the tree and moved parallel to the road. Glazer knew that the man was trying to see the back of the property, if there was anything behind the house that he should be concerned about. The man found a new position and watched for a long time. Glazer kept his eyes on him. Eventually the man pulled back into the depths of the woods and was gone.

"Nathaniel was such a sweet boy when he was young," Mary finally said. "Called me momma, kissed me on the cheek every morning. Picked wildflowers, brought them to me. How does such a thing happen?"

"I don't know."

"Sometimes I think he was corrupted somehow, that someone got their hands on him and reached in and twisted him all up inside. Did something to his soul. But I know that ain't true. It was always there, from the moment he was born. I should've seen it."

"It's no one's fault but his own," Glazer said.

"That's only partly true, though, isn't it?"

"This isn't about assigning blame one way or another."

"No, it's about something far worse." Mary started to rock again, the back of the chair banging against the house. "I used to go and see a traveling preacher. He'd set up his tent on the other side of town and deliver the gospel from morning until night for a week or so. Would come around a couple times a year. He'd talk a lot about the Lord's forgiveness, how it was absolute. But you had to seek it. You had to seek it. And if you didn't, then the only thing awaiting you was the pit."

"I'm not concerned about that."

"None of that frightens you?"

"I know where I'm going when this is all done. And I won't be alone. The men that did the things they did to my family will be there as well, and I'll be waiting for them."

"This is never going to end, is it?"

"No. It is not."

Glazer stared at the woods across the road. The shadows between the trees deepened and widened as the sun moved across the sky and it appeared as if the shadows were twisting to life, dashing and darting over the ground, stretching out between the trees.

5.

As the afternoon headed toward night the hotel lobby came alive with people, most of them men covered in dirt and sweat, returning from the fields and looking for some supper. When darkness began to take hold, a woman in a flowing dress walked around the lobby, lighting the lanterns that hung on the walls. At one time the lanterns had been ornate, but now they were old and chipped and covered with a thin layer of grime. The piano sat alone, covered with a gray piece of thin cloth. The area behind the counter had been cleaned up.

In the aftermath of the gunfight, Eli had showed the proprietor Lee's badge and claimed that Lee was a fugitive that he and his partner had been tracking. The young man stood next to the proprietor and looked like he was going to say something, but Eli gave the young man a look and he was quiet. The proprietor complained about the damage to his bar and Eli slipped him several greasy bills and the proprietor smiled and said he was happy to help however he could. The first few men who came in looked around at the damage with uncertainty but that quickly faded. Once you've seen war, it took more than a few bullet holes to get and hold your attention.

The three of them sat at a table, Eli and Bobby drinking whiskey. Lee sat between them, his leg now wrapped with linen. The young man kept bringing him tea and Lee slowly drank it, glass after glass. Eli had searched him for other weapons, but he didn't find the knife. Lee felt it pressing down onto the side of his foot. He could have it up and out of the boot within a second or two.

When Bobby had returned, he grunted for nearly a minute and finished by holding up two fingers. Lee hadn't understood what he meant, but Eli had. Samuel was with an old woman. There was no one else there, but they were still going to wait until it got dark. The road out there was used fairly regularly, and they didn't want anyone around.

Once the sun was completely set and the street out front was dark, Bobby stood and went outside. Eli nudged Lee, who slowly climbed to his feet, favoring his injured left leg. Eli walked over to the counter and spoke with the proprietor, handed him another small wad of greasy money. Lee limped toward the door. The young man stood near the piano, acting like he was sweeping up some scraps of wood. He caught Lee's eye and knelt and opened a small piece of cloth. Inside of it was a pistol. It looked like a LeMat. The young man gestured for Lee to take it. Lee looked the young man in the eyes and shook his head, a sad smile on his face. He appreciated the gesture, but if he went for the gun it was just going to get a lot of people killed. The young man frowned and quickly tucked the gun away and went back to his sweeping. Lee turned to the door and went out.

Bobby had Lee's horse near the steps. Lee hobbled over to it and Bobby held it steady while he climbed up. Eli came out, still holding the Henry. He and his brother climbed onto their horses and the three of them rode south, toward the train tracks, Lee between them.

"That place had some fine whiskey," Eli said. "You should've had yourself a glass."

"I don't drink."

"Like that matters at this point."

"It matters to me."

"Suit yourself."

The road was dark and they traveled three abreast, the brothers keeping Lee between them. Lee's horse snorted and gnashed, but when Lee pressed his feet into its sides it quieted down. During the war Lee had faced death nearly every day, but it was always something of an abstraction, a threat that might or might not ever come to pass. But now it was certain. His life was measured in minutes and he felt the world fading away from him, the road, the dark trees, even the night sky no longer looked as it should. It was if the world knew what was about to transpire and was already withdrawing.

Lee stole a glance at Bobby. He was to the left of Lee and was looking straight ahead. Lee shifted and grunted, moved the weight off of his injured leg. He felt blood dribble down his shin. Eli was to Lee's right. He had a smile on his face.

He knew the brothers would kill him before they reached the Keller farm. Better to die here on this dusty road than be left whimpering in some ditch. Lee moved faster than he could think and pulled the knife out of his boot. He planted all his weight on the right stirrup and lunged toward Eli, the knife leading the way.

The knife went in smooth, right below Eli's left clavicle. Lee's body hit Eli with his full weight and the two of them tumbled to the ground, the knife pushed in all the way to the hilt. Eli shouted as they fell and Lee heard Bobby grunt in surprise. Lee and Eli hit the ground and Lee released the knife and went for Eli's pistol. Eli punched Lee in the side of the head and brought up a knee in an attempt to get Lee off of him.

From behind him, Lee heard Bobby cock the Sharps.

Lee grabbed Eli by the throat and rolled away from Bobby, pulling Eli up so that if Bobby fired he'd hit his brother. Eli screamed and opened his mouth and bit one of Lee's hands. They tumbled through the darkness and Lee grabbed the knife and pulled it out. He raised the knife and the Sharps fired and the bullet went through Lee's palm, right through the meat beneath the thumb. He dropped the knife and was up and running as fast as his injured leg would carry him. A bullet snapped past his head and he plunged into the darkness of the woods.

Eli slowly climbed to his feet. Placed a hand on the wound in his chest. "Goddamn," he said. "That is one tenacious motherfucker."

Bobby grunted and rode toward the edge of the woods, the Sharps up and ready.

"Let him be," Eli said. "Between his leg and hand, he won't get far." Eli walked over to Lee's horse, took its reins, and tied them to the horn on his saddle. "Probably end up bleeding to death out there in the woods."

Bobby moved his horse back and forth along the edge of the road, still watching the darkness. Eli rode past. "Let's go," he said.

Bobby took a last look at the woods and fell in behind his brother.

6.

Kate and Jeremiah sat at the kitchen table. Jeremiah read one of his books and Kate sipped a cup of coffee and flipped through an old periodical. The periodical was from England and nearly fifteen years old, crumbling and yellowed. She didn't know why she kept it, probably because of the drawings of the English countryside and the stories that detailed how they lived. It all seemed so romantic, so proper. Everything had its place and nothing ever seemed to change that.

Jeremiah closed his book and yawned. He looked at the dark kitchen window and got up, the book under one arm. "I'm tired, Momma."

"Sleep in my bed tonight," Kate said.

"Yes, ma'am." Jeremiah crossed the kitchen and headed for his room. "I'm going to change into my nightshirt."

"I'll be in there in a minute so we can say your prayers." Kate watched Jeremiah for a moment then returned to the periodical. She flipped through to the end, not interested in any of the pages dedicated to sewing. After finishing the last of her coffee, she got up and placed the empty cup onto the counter near the stove. She was just turning to check on Jeremiah when she heard the rattling of a carriage and then someone started to beat on the back door.

"Open the door, Kate," a man's voice said.

She stood still for a moment. Anger burned through her and when there was another loud knock on the back door, she quickly walked into her bedroom. Jeremiah sat on the bed, his shirt off. Kate grabbed the shotgun off of the bureau.

"What is it, Momma?"

"You stay in here, understand?"

Jeremiah nodded.

The beating on the back door continued and Kate walked back through the house and onto the back porch. She cocked the shotgun. "Whoever's out there, you have five seconds to get off my property. I have a gun."

There was a moment of silence from outside and then Hansford spoke. "Do not make this harder than it needs to be, Kate."

"I will shoot you if you step foot in this house," Kate said. She took a step back and aimed the shotgun at the back door. "I swear to God, I will."

From outside came the mumbled voices of several men. There was a shout and the back door splintered and broke apart, shards of wood flying through the air. Kate instinctively ducked and fired one wild shot that struck the roof of the back porch. Two huge men smashed through the last of the back door with a large log. They stormed onto the back porch and wrestled the shotgun away from Kate. She fought and screamed and one of them punched her in the chest and she fell back into the kitchen, struggling to breathe.

Hansford stepped onto the back porch, flanked by four other men. "It's time for you to come home."

Kate lay on the floor, gasping for breath, as one of the men reached down and took her by the arms. Jeremiah charged into the kitchen, holding the pistol. Jeremiah fired and hit one of the men in the leg. The man dropped and one of the other men pulled out his pistol and shot Jeremiah twice in the chest. The boy stumbled backward and crashed into the table before he fell to the floor, blood spreading out around his body.

Kate looked at her dead son and screamed. Large, rough hands lifted her up and carried her outside. The men took her toward the road and she kicked and screamed, thrashed as hard as she could, but they were too strong. They tossed her into the back of Hansford's carriage. She wailed and tried to get out and one of the men punched her in the face. She fell back onto the seat and Hansford climbed in. He slapped the side of the carriage and it started down the road and Kate looked at her house, at the dark figures surrounding it. One of the men lit a torch and threw it onto the back porch. Fire erupted out of the windows and smoke spindled up from the roof. Kate screamed and screamed but there was no one to hear her.

7.

Glazer shot Mary just as the sun was going down. He helped her change into a different dress and got her into bed. He placed the picture of Jesus Christ on her chest and put the Colt against her forehead. She closed her eyes and mumbled something only she could hear. He pulled the trigger. Afterwards he covered her with a sheet.

He stood there for a long time, looking down at her. Her only sin was giving birth to a monster, but it was sin enough. He pulled out the piece of paper and crossed Nathanial Keller's name from the list and put the paper back into his breast pocket. He flipped open the Colt, added a round to it, and went out back to his horse.

The horse stood still in the tall grass and Glazer grabbed the saddle and strapped it onto the horse's back. It was now full dark and the moon was barely out. The stench from the outhouse drifted like a fog across the back of the property. Glazer led the horse away from the house and tied it to a tree. He wanted it to be out of sight. He took his Spencer and crossed back to the house, but instead of going in, he skirted the collapsed section and followed it around to the front. He crouched in the darkness and waited.

An hour or so later, two men moved silently through the woods across the road. Glazer watched them. The men settled in near a large tree, one on either side of it, and they sat there for several minutes before one of the men, the one that Glazer had seen earlier, moved away from the tree and crept down to the road. The man was bent low, a pistol in one hand. The other man stayed at the tree. He held a rifle that was sighted in on the door.

The man coming toward the house ran across the road and took up position near the gate. Even in the dark Glazer saw that the man's face was ruined and that he wore a bandanna to cover it. Glazer watched him, set his position, and looked back across the road. The man near the tree had shifted his position and now the rifle was aimed at Glazer. He raised the Spencer but the man with the rifle shot first and the bullet struck Glazer right below his heart. Glazer crashed to the ground, his rifle skittering away from him.

He lay there for a moment and reached up and felt the wound. There was no pain. He struggled to sit up, fingers still feeling the edges of the bullet hole. There was no blood. He looked down at his chest in partial amazement.

Before he could move, the man with the ruined face was on him.

He kicked Glazer in the head and Glazer spun around, onto his stomach. His fingers dug into the ground for purchase and as he fought to get back to his feet, the man shot him three times in the back at close range, each round striking him like a hammer. Glazer's vision faded in and out and he couldn't tell if his eyes were open or closed. A weight descended upon him.

From the road came the footsteps of the other man.

"He dead?" one of the men said.

The other one grunted.

"Let's see what's inside," one of the men said. There was a scuffling sound as they walked away. The front door banged as they entered the house.

A wave of darkness struck Glazer and swept him away. He fell through a dark, endless void, his body tumbling out of control, arms and legs flailing. From somewhere came the faint sound of approaching footsteps, hundreds of them, and with each passing moment they grew louder and louder. He opened his eyes and found himself back where he started, in front of the house, near the road. He was surrounded on all sides by an endless gathering of the dead. Men, women, children, of all races and colors, their pale eyes staring at him.

He sat up and looked at them. Some were little more than skeletons with bits of dried flesh hanging from their bones, while others could still have passed for the living. They all stared at him, an unrelenting, unanimous gaze of pain and sorrow and hate, and he understood. For the first time, he truly understood.

A woman dressed only in a tattered and torn blouse stepped forward. The inside of her legs were streaked with blood and she bent down and picked up the Spencer. She held it gingerly, with both hands, and walked over to Glazer and handed it to him. He took it and looked at the woman and she simply stared back, the whites of her eyes a formless emptiness. Glazer climbed to his feet and walked toward the front of the house, the dead filling the road behind him.

The two men were in the kitchen, tearing into anything that wasn't nailed down. Glazer quietly entered through the front door and started toward them. As he walked past Mary he looked at her and saw that they had tossed her from the bed. Her body lay sprawled out on the dirty floor, eyes open, one arm bent beneath her. The sheets were everywhere and the old mattress lay cockeyed off the frame. The picture of Jesus Christ smashed on the floor.

The man with the ruined face turned and saw Glazer. Even with his wasted features, it was evident that the man was shocked. Glazer raised the Spencer and shot him twice in the face. He stumbled backwards and crashed into the back door and fell out into the night.

The other man ducked behind the table and fired twice, one round striking Glazer in the left arm, the other in the neck. Glazer stormed forward and kicked the table directly into the man, knocking him back. The man dropped the rifle and Glazer raised his gun and fired three times into the man's chest.

Glazer looked around the kitchen. The air smelled of copper and powder and smoke clung to the ceiling. He lowered his gun and returned to Mary. He reassembled the bed and placed her on top of it. He picked up the picture of Christ and looked at it. The frame was destroyed and part of the picture was torn near the bottom, but otherwise it was intact. Christ's eyes looked gently toward the heaven of the picture and Glazer ran a finger over those eyes and placed the picture on Mary's chest. He got the sheet and covered her with it.

He walked around the house, taking in the destruction. He flipped over the kitchen table and returned it to its proper place before grabbing the dead man by the hands and dragging him out of the kitchen and placing him on the ground near the other man. Glazer went back in and straightened out what could still be straightened. Once he was satisfied, he went outside and took each man by a hand and pulled them away from the house, leaving them next to the outhouse. After one last look around, he went to his horse.

He led it out onto the road, which was now quiet and empty, and climbed up into the saddle. He brought the horse to a gallop, once again headed south, and the night swallowed him completely.

§

Lee stood in the house, looking at the covered woman on the bed. He pulled back the sheet and saw the bullet hole in her head, the picture of Jesus Christ on her chest. He put the sheet back and hobbled toward the back of the house. He found his Henry sitting on the table. He picked it up and went outside.

It was first light and he found the bodies out by the outhouse. Both had been shot multiple times and bloat and rot was starting to take control of their faces. He bent and went through their belts, pulling out all the rounds he could find. He took Eli's holster and wrapped it around himself and put Eli's Colt in it.

He found the pump and got the water going. He took a drink and let the water settle into his stomach before holding his injured hand under the cold water. Lee dug at the wound with a thumb, worked off all the grime that had started to take root. Once the wound was clear it started to bleed and he let it, leaning against the pump, the blood running off his hand.

After washing the wound a second time, he slowly made his way back into the house and dug through a cupboard in the kitchen. He found some towels and he tore them into strips and wrapped his hand. The cloth near the wound turned a light red. He sat on the floor and removed the linen from where he'd been shot in the leg. The hole in the front was a bright red. He couldn't the see the back of the leg, but it felt clean. He tore up the rest of the towels and re-wrapped his leg.

He took one last look around the house before walking out through the front door and closing it behind him. His horse was tied to the fence near the road and he hobbled toward it. He'd taken everything there was worth taking from Bobby and Eli's horses and left them tied at the side of the road so someone would find them. It didn't seem right to just turn them loose.

Lee climbed up onto his horse and looked at the road. There was nothing keeping him from returning home. He could head north and within a week or so be back home with his wife and child. There was still the issue of Hansford and the shop, but Lee could deal with him. If he had to, he'd sell his land for whatever he could get and they'd move away, maybe to Ohio or even Nebraska. It all seemed so simple. But these things were never easy. There was always something tugging at a man's soul, an internal compass that showed him the path he was meant to follow, whether he wanted to or not.

The rising sun chased the shadows from the road and Lee knew that Samuel, if that was his real name, wouldn't stop. He'd move on to the next name and either kill that man or that man's family. Regardless of what had been done, the atrocities those men carried out, their families didn't have anything to do with it. They didn't deserve the fate that awaited them and if Lee didn't do anything to stop what was coming, he was no better than Eli or Bobby. Just another immoral man wandering an immoral world.

He brought his horse up onto the road and started south. He'd find someone to tell him how to find the Abbott plantation and once this was all done with, he'd send Kate a telegram and let her know he was on his way back home.

MONDAY

1.

Glazer stood on the side of the road, talking to his horse. The saddle and panniers lay discarded on the side of the road. The sun was low in the western sky and thick shadows were starting to consume the landscape.

The horse rubbed its nose against Glazer's forehead and he felt its breath. Warm and wet. He rubbed it between the ears and felt sorrow that it had been forced to endure all of this. That it had been forced to follow the same path he was condemned to walk. Glazer lowered his hands and let the horse go. It looked at him, its eyes soft and brown. He reached up and touched its neck one last time and turned and started down the middle of the road. When he looked back, the horse was gone.

All he carried was his rifle. In his shirt pocket, next to the list, was the advertisement with the woman. After finding Walter Nail's family in Alabama, he had considered getting rid of it. Tearing it to pieces or even burning it. But he decided against it. That woman was as much a part of him as anything else, and she'd be there until the end.

The Abbott plantation was a mile or so away, set off from the road by a wide lane. He walked toward it in the growing darkness. Glazer reached the lane and turned onto it, the Spencer in his hands. He could see the main house, ringed as it was by torches. Men darted here and there and Glazer knew that someone had warned Abbott, told him what was coming for him. Glazer cocked the Spencer.

A wagon sat parked about twenty feet in front of the main porch, a torch in the front, near the seat. Three men used the wagon as cover and as soon as they saw Glazer, they opened fire. The bullets punched into his legs and chest and arms and he continued on. He raised the Spencer and fired. The head of one man vanished in a spray of red. The remaining two men ran for the house and Glazer shot them in the back.

The remaining men scattered and took up positions along the length of the front porch. They sighted in on Glazer and opened fire.

§

From the back of the house, Lee heard the rolling tide of gunfire. He was in the kitchen with Matthew Abbott, his wife Cynthia, and their three young boys. Lee's leg was still heavily wrapped but he could move freely. Four of Abbott's men, each armed with a rifle and two pistols stood guard. Two at the back door and two at the doorway that led to the dining room. From the doorway they had a clear view all the way through the house.

"Sounds like the men out there are giving him hell," Abbott said.

"Let's just wait here and see what happens." Lee had been with the Abbotts for two weeks now. At first Matthew hadn't believed what Lee was telling him, that a man was tracking down and killing anyone involved with what had happened at the little farm outside of Fayette. But Matthew had kept in touch with Walter Nail's wife, had sent her money to help care for her four girls. A week ago, at Lee's urging, he sent a telegram to check on her. It was two days before he received a reply.

Mrs. Walter Nail and her girls had been at a wedding. Right in the middle of the ceremony a man walked into the church and opened fire. Two of the Nail girls went down. As the man aimed his gun at Mrs. Nail, he was shot several times by three men at the back of the church, at least once in the head. The man turned and shot the three men, one after another, like bottles on a fence. In the end Mrs. Nail and her last two girls were caught in the small cemetery behind the church. He shot them point-blank. The preacher put at least three rounds into the man's back, but the man didn't even turn around. He simply stood there looking down at Mrs. Nail and her girls before vanishing into the woods on the far side of the cemetery.

The gunfire from outside subsided and a scream drifted through the house. The men at the doorway looked back at Abbott. "Stay where you are," he said.

"If he's not dead yet," Lee said, "we're not going to be able to stop him."

"He's not getting to my family," Abbott said. He turned to Cynthia and looked at her. Their boys were clustered around their mother, hands clutching the folds of her dress.

"He'll come in the front, down that hallway and into the dining room," Lee said. "If he makes it that far, take your family out the back door. Try and get to the wagon."

"You think I'm running like a goddamn coward? I will not abandon my home."

Lee glared at Abbott. "Don't let your family die because of your pride."

Abbott looked at his wife. Tears ran down her face, but her hands slid over the heads of her children, trying to soothe them.

"If I go, you're coming with me," Abbott said to Lee. "Anything happens to me, you'll protect them."

"You have my word," Lee said. He walked over to the doorway and looked across the dining room, toward the front of the house. His uninjured hand held the Colt. His other hand was still wrapped and he raised it and touched the telegram in his shirt pocket. When he first arrived, he had sent a telegram to Kate telling her that she didn't have anything to worry about, that he'd be home soon. That when he got back they'd figure out what they were going to do. Her reply came an hour or so later. Both her and Jeremiah were fine and were eager for him to be home.

§

Glazer walked toward the front porch, bullets tearing into him. His shirt was nearly gone, the cloth shredded, his skin pockmarked from bullet wounds. None of them bled.

A man near the front door raised his rifle and pulled the trigger. There was nothing save for a useless click. The man cursed. He threw the rifle at Glazer and went for his pistol. Glazer shot him in the throat.

From the end of the porch came two gunshots. Glazer turned and fired, striking one man in the head and the other in the leg. The second man started to scream. Glazer pulled a cartridge for the Spencer from his belt and put it in place. The man continued to scream. The ground in front of the porch was littered with bodies.

Glazer kicked open the front door to the house and went in.

§

All four of Abbott's men were at the doorway, two on each side, one low, one high. They fired on the man walking across the dining room.

"We need to leave," Lee said to Abbott.

Abbott cocked his rifle. "I'm not going anywhere."

"He'll kill you. You, me, Cynthia. The boys."

"Then he'll kill me." One of the men by the door was shot in the head. He crumbled to the floor, his rifle still clutched in one hand. Abbott looked at Lee. "Get them out of here. There's a root cellar behind the cotton barn, you'll see the mound. Good a place as any to hole up."

"You can't leave us, Matthew!" Cynthia said. "Please!"

Abbott checked his gun to make sure it was loaded. "I'm not the man you think I am," he said. "I never was. But if I die here, maybe he'll leave you and the boys alone. Maybe I'll be enough."

"I'm begging you!" Cynthia said. "We can get to the wagon, escape all this."

"There's no escaping this." Abbott looked at Lee. "Get them the hell out of here."

Two more of the men at the doorway went down. The last one stood and charged into the dining room. There were two quick shots and then the only sound was the echo of boots striking the wooden floor, incessant, pounding. Heavy.

Lee grabbed Cynthia and led her and the children out the back door and into the night. He looked back and saw Abbott lift his gun and fire.

§

A man stood in the kitchen, firing his weapon at Glazer. Glazer knew that his name was Abbott. That he was the one who had shot William.

Glazer grabbed Abbott by the throat and pulled him close. Abbott's eyes were wild with rage and he tried to yell, but all that came out was spit. Glazer placed the barrel of his rifle beneath Abbott's chin and pulled the trigger.

From behind Glazer came the sensation of pure cold. Cold so deep it burned. He turned. The dining room and the hallway beyond was filled with the dead. In front was the woman with the bloody inner legs, the one who had returned his rifle. The dead didn't move but he felt them reaching for him, beckoning for him to join them. But he wasn't ready. Something primal and insatiable unspooled inside of him, a hunger unlike any he had ever known. And he was not going to stop until it was satisfied.

He turned his back on the dead and went outside.

§

Cynthia and the boys reached the root cellar first. One of the boys threw open the storm doors and went down, grabbing a lantern that hung just inside the doorway. He handed it to his mother, who pulled out a match and lit it. She stood to one side and the boys filed past her, vanishing in the dark below.

Lee stood a few feet in front of the root cellar. He had a clear view of the back of the house.

"Is he coming?"

"I'll do everything I can to protect you and your boys," Lee said.

"Why are you doing this?"

Lee thought for a moment, his eyes tracking the man. He was about twenty feet from the back door, was walking toward them slowly and deliberately. "Maybe because some things can't go unchallenged."

Cynthia nodded and went into the cellar. Lee closed the doors behind her and waited for the man to reach him.

§

Glazer walked across the back of the property, surrounded on all sides by the dead. Men, women, children, the elderly. All witnesses to unspeakable acts and all of them bearing scars and wounds that would never heal.

As Glazer walked toward the man standing in front of the earth mound, the dead started to move toward him, like a wave collapsing in on itself. Glazer felt a pull from somewhere deep within himself and he fought it off. He would not stop. Not now. Not ever.

Cold descended upon him, blew in from the fields of the dead, and the cold caught fire and engulfed his body. The flames were blue and white and heavy. He felt them slowing him down, his weight increasing with each step he took. The dead pushed forward and he thought of his wife, hanging from the rafters, her skin peeling off. Of the day he met her. The day she married him. The day she made him a father. His son dead out in the weeds, his son the doctor. He loved them more than anything in existence and knew he would never see them again. All he had left were their names and faces. The dead pushing in on him would be his only companions. From this point in time to the end of time.

The air smelled of frost and sorrow and eternity. Glazer raised his gun and advanced on the man standing in front of the root cellar.

§

Lee pushed an old cart out away from the storm doors, positioning it so that there was plenty of space between him and the root cellar. It didn't provide much cover, but it'd have to do. There was nothing else.

The man walking toward him raised his rifle and started to fire.

Lee ducked down behind the cart. Bullets tore into it, blew chunks of wood and dust into the air. Lee went to move down to the other end of the cart and pain erupted from his injured leg. He looked at it, saw the dressing turning dark. Another volley of shots plowed into the cart.

Lee closed his eyes and took a breath. Felt his lungs inflate. Then he stood and returned fire.

§

The dead were all around Glazer now, their hands and arms and mouths reaching out for him. The flames spread across Glazer's face and the world turned blue, like he was looking at it through a sheet of thick ice. The cold was unbearable. An old woman, her desiccated face lacking eyes, latched onto Glazer's back and she climbed up. He was surrounded by wailing. Screaming. He was almost to the man, almost to the woman and children hiding beneath the ground. All he needed was a few more moments. He would not be denied.

§

Lee reloaded and stood and fired three times. All three rounds struck the man in the chest and he didn't slow. The man returned fire and Lee was hit in the chest and the stomach. He went down hard, his injured leg breaking beneath him. He screamed from the pain and his gun dropped from his hands. Lee had never known such pain.

The man stopped next to the cart and looked down at Lee. Lee's eyes slid in and out of focus. He didn't know how much longer he would be able to see. The man walked toward the storm doors, back bent like someone was hanging off of him. Lee crawled forward and got his injured leg out from under him. The man was going for the second storm door. Lee looked around and saw his pistol a few feet away.

He crawled toward the gun, hand outstretched toward it.

§

The dead swarmed Glazer, hung on his legs, clung to his back, fingers and nails digging for purchase on whatever they could grasp. The flames grew colder, more ferocious. From behind him came a roaring sound. It sounded like a train, of screaming metal and steam. But he knew it wasn't a train. There were no words for what was coming for him. The air turned rotten. Glazer held his gun in one hand and with the other struggled to open the second door to the cellar. He looked down into the cellar, saw the dim light of a lantern, a woman standing at the foot of the steps, a shovel held up like a weapon. The woman's face was covered in dirt.

The sound of the train grew louder.

§

Lee reached his gun and he picked it up, his fingers moving impossibly slow. He rolled onto his back in time to see the man toss open the second door. The man took a step down onto the stairs and Lee raised his gun and fired. The bullet struck the man in the head. The man turned and stared at Lee, a look of surprise on his face. Lee shot the man in the throat. The man waved a hand at something that wasn't there before raising the rifle and aiming it at Lee. The man pulled the trigger, but the cartridge was empty.

Lee fired again and struck the man in the chest. The man tossed aside the rifle, pulled out a knife, and started toward Lee.

The man dropped onto Lee, pinned him to the ground. Lee raised the pistol and fired, but the shot went wide and the man knocked the gun from his hand. The man's eyes were black and deep and something swirled in the void beyond them. He brought down the knife and Lee raised his hands and grabbed the man's wrist, used what little strength he had left to slow the knife's descent. The man pushed down and the knife inched closer to Lee's throat.

§

Everywhere Glazer looked, all he saw was blue fire. His arms and legs were so cold they no longer had any feeling. The sound of the train grew louder and closer and now he heard it for what it was, millions of voices, each screaming in unison. He knew it was coming for him, coming for what was owed. What was promised.

The dead were everywhere.

He pressed down and the blade of the knife reached the man's throat. The man stared at Glazer. The man's eyes were brown and clear.

"The woman and children down there," the man said, his voice weak and dry. "They're innocent."

"No one is innocent," Glazer said, but for the first time in a long time he didn't believe it. The blue flames erupted outward and started to spread among the dead, moving from body to body. None of them moved. Glazer looked at them. At the grief and rage on their faces.

"Kill me," the man mumbled. "Kill me and let them be."

"You'd do such a thing?" Glazer said. But he already knew the answer. The blue flames cut a wide berth around the man. Glazer was cold, colder than he could even imagine was possible. He pressed the knife down into the man's neck and blood slipped out. The dead moved forward and reached out to Glazer and he let them claim him.

§

There was a strange pressure in Lee's throat and when he tried to swallow nothing happened. The pain faded away and he felt like he was suspended, something else carrying all of his weight.

A woman appeared at his side and somehow he knew her. She was doing something to his neck, her hands bloody and slick, and she was yelling, screaming, wanting to know where the other man had gone. He had no answer for her. She continued to scream, but he no longer cared what she had to say and as the woman faded away it occurred to him that dying made a mockery of life, that something so important should not be so fragile.

SATURDAY

*T*he young man with the green cap walks down the middle of the road. It is full dark and there is no one around. Even the insects are quiet. The man hums to himself as he walks, his boots scraping across the top of the hard, dry dirt.

On the edge of the small town two men hang from opposite sides of a tall tree, ropes creaking from their weight. The skinny man's body is still and straight, like a candle, but the other man's large body is flush and bloated, his shirt ripped into strips. One of his arms looks like it was broken and his right eye is swollen shut. He had fought to the very end. The young man walks over to the hanged man and touches his foot. Emory. His name had been Emory. Emory and Paul.

He takes one last look at the two men and continues on, through town. The tavern is nearly full and he hears the clinking of glasses and muffled yelling. He doesn't look at the tavern as he goes by. There's nothing in there to see that he hasn't seen countless times before.

He follows a road out of town and before long he reaches a wide drive that leads to a plantation. He can see the main house from the road and he stops and watches it. The air is still and thick and fireflies silently drift through the air. He smells cotton and cut grass and wildflowers. He starts for the house.

Two white men sit on the porch. Both are armed and one is whittling a piece of wood, shaping it into a recorder of some type, the mouthpiece crooked. He walks past them and neither of them see him. He passes through the door and is inside.

The inside of the house is spacious and clean. He stands in a large atrium, a chandelier of candles hanging from the ceiling, which is flanked on both sides by a winding staircase. The floor is smooth and the inside of the house smells of fresh paint. From somewhere in the back comes the sound of a man talking.

He walks across the atrium toward the sound of the talking and passes through a sitting room before continuing on down a long, wide hallway. Portraits line both walls, faces of men that all share vague similarities in their facial features. He pauses and takes them in, looking at *each one in turn.*

A small dog comes down the hallway toward him. It stops and growls. The young man smiles at the dog and bends down and offers it a hand. The dog barks twice, tail between its legs, before it turns and runs back the way it came.

The hallway ends in a dining room and a man and a woman sit at the table, near each other, plates of food sitting in front of them. In the middle of the table is a cooked duck. It is flanked by a bowl of green beans and a plate of grilled potatoes and a sweating pitcher of water.

The woman is done up in a cream colored lace dress with pearls inlaid around the collar. The man wears a white suit, his mustache shimmering from the wax that helps it keep its shape. The woman stares at her plate, not moving. The man talks to her as if all of this was natural. As if they had already spent the entirety of their lives together.

The young man walks over to the table and smells the duck. A servant comes into the dining room, a plate of biscuits in one hand, but the man at the table shoos her away. The young man walks around the table and stops next to the woman and waits.

The man at the table continues to talk, about the duck and how hard it was to raise, about the war, about how the cotton is coming in, about how the niggers that wanted to be free have all returned to work for next to nothing. It's aimless talk meant to fill the silence and nothing more.

The woman stays still for the longest time. Then she screams and snatches up her knife and lunges toward the man in the white suit. She stabs him in the shoulder, the knife sinking to the hilt and he yells in pain and rises up and punches her in the chest. She falls to the floor. Her eyes are wild, like an unhinged animal, and she snarls and gets up, still holding the knife.

The young man watches all of this and waits.

She slashes at the man, but he's expecting another attack and is able to keep away from her. The woman screams and charges and plows into the man and they both crash to the floor. He fights her, tries to hold her hands, keep her from stabbing him. Her mouth hangs open in a scream and two other men charge into the room and the man in the white suit yells at them to get her off of him. They both go for her, but she swipes the knife at them and catches one in the chest. The man goes down, bleeding.

The young man walks around the end of the table and watches.

The second man pulls out a gun and tells her that he's going to shoot, that he's going to blow her goddamned head off. The woman snarls and screams, her pupils so wide that they nearly cover the whites of her eyes. She leaps to her feet and charges the man with the gun. The man in the white suit yells to shoot, to kill her before she inflicts more harm. The second man fires and the bullet strikes her in the neck and she tumbles to the floor, choking on her own blood. The knife slides away from her outstretched hand.

The man in the white suit gets up, one hand on his bleeding shoulder, and he looks down at the woman and curses her, tells her that she brought all of this on herself, that none of this had to happen.

She looks up at him, her eyes slowly blinking. The man in the white suit snorts and curses and tells the man with the gun to get rid of her. To dump her out in the woods. That's the best she deserves.

The man holsters his gun and picks her up under the armpits and drags her out through the back of the house. The young man takes one last look around the dining room and follows. The three of them walk across the backyard, toward a thick stand of trees that borders the cotton. The woman struggles to breathe.

When they're deep in the trees, the man drops her next to an old elm tree and walks away without looking back.

The young man hears her gasping for breath and he walks over to her and bends down and places a hand on her forehead.

She looks up at him. The fury still burns in her eyes but it's growing dimmer. He bends so that his mouth is near her ear and he whispers to her, tells her that her husband is dead, murdered somewhere down in Georgia, that her son's body lies half-buried under the smoldering ruins of her house. And there it is going to remain, on that foul, unconsecrated ground.

There is no justice in this world, he says. None at all. The people who deserve to be punished rarely are, that people forget other's crimes when it's convenient for them to forget and that those crimes stay forgotten. And if she's forgotten, who will see justice done for her and her family? The men who tried to fight for her are already dead, hanging from an old tree. Two good men out of an entire town. Two men.

This world deserves to burn, he tells her.

She turns her face and looks at him. Her cheeks are pale and her lips are fast losing their color. He whispers to her that he can help her change all of that, that he can give her the means to bring the wicked to justice. The means to make all of them suffer and burn for what they've done.

A tear slides down her face and she asks if she does this, will she see her family again? He tells her no, that there is always a price to pay. And that is hers.

She closes her eyes and he knows she's filling her mind with the images of her husband, of her son, so that they will carry her through what's to come. When she opens them, she looks the young man in the eyes and nods. He reaches over and takes her hand and smiles, but it's not a smile of joy or warmth or celebration. It's a smile of grief and anger and vengeance, a smile that acknowledges the coming storm. The horror on the precipice of being unleashed.

He holds her hand until she draws her last breath. When she has gone silent, he pulls a piece of blank paper out of his left breast pocket, folds it in half, and places it in her cold right hand. He stands and takes one last look at her before leaving her there, her body cooling beneath the canopy of trees, beneath the dark night sky, beneath the umbrella of rage and hopelessness and injustice that pollutes the world.

The End

Acknowledgements

This story wouldn't exist without the following people:

My wife, Cindy, who supported me every step of the way.

Matt Wise, who endlessly championed it to anyone who would listen.

Sean Cleveland, whose generosity I can never repay.

Very special thanks to Tim Bradstreet for the amazing cover art, Rob Ozborne for his hard work on the cover design, and to Krissy Roleke for her keen copyediting eye.

Several others read early drafts and provided invaluable feedback. They are Jan Fischer-Wade, Li Kuo, Dan Morris, Chuck Osborn, Adam Gomolin, and Don Poole.

I thank all of them for their time and support.

William Harms has written for Marvel Comics, DC Comics, Image Comics, Top Cow, Sony Computer Entertainment, and 2K. He was the lead writer on Mafia III, which was widely acclaimed for its narrative and was nominated for several writing awards, including a British Academy Film and Television Arts (BAFTA) Games Award.

His graphic novel series Impaler was nominated for an International Horror Guild Award.

He resides in Northern California with his wife and cat. You can reach him at www.williamharms.com or on Twitter @wjharms.

CPSIA information can be obtained
at www.ICGtesting.com
Printed in the USA
LVHW010225200620
658570LV00013B/1769